Allocating Annie

A Comedy in Two Acts

Rick Abbot

A SAMUEL FRENCH ACTING EDITION

SAMUEL FRENCH

FOUNDED 1830

SAMUELFRENCH.COM
SAMUELFRENCH-LONDON.CO.UK

FOR PRODUCTION ENQUIRIES

UNITED STATES AND CANADA
Info@SamuelFrench.com
1-866-598-8449

UNITED KINGDOM AND EUROPE
Theatre@SamuelFrench-London.co.uk
020-7255-4302

Each title is subject to availability from Samuel French, depending upon country of performance. Please be aware that *ALLOCATING ANNIE* may not be licensed by Samuel French in your territory. Professional and amateur producers should contact the nearest Samuel French office or licensing partner to verify availability.

"ALLOCATING ANNIE"

—Cast of Characters—

CLIFFORD TUCKER, an eminent plastic surgeon
TRACY TUCKER, his sister and housekeeper
JAKE PUTNAM, his lawyer and best friend
LANGDON BARNETT, an aspiring actor
ANNABEL FESCO, an unexpected visitor
BOBBI RALSTON, a sexy lady anthropologist
REBECCA RALSTON, Bobbi's wealthy mother

Setting: Clifford's luxurious Manhattan condominium

Time: about mid-January at its snowy worst

ACT ONE: a momentous morning in mid-week

ACT TWO: that evening about 6 o'clock

Allocating Annie

ACT ONE

Curtain rises on the posh Manhattan apartment of DR. CLIFFORD TUCKER. [see Stage Setting] The facades of tall and elegant buildings can be seen through the floor-to-ceiling picture window in the foyer — mostly the tops of these buildings, so we know this apartment is on a highly wealthy level. Though it is mid-January, the day outside is, for the moment, bright and sunny with that extra-keen winter brightness. There is a place-setting for one at L. side of dining table, minus only the plate itself. A moment after curtain-rise, TRACY TUCKER Enters from kitchen [for convenience, let's call the D.S. kitchen doorway K.D. and the kitchen doorway in the R.C. wall K.R.] via K.D., bearing a plate with a hot breakfast — bacon, eggs, hash-browns, whatever — and a small tray holding a coffeepot. She sets these on table, then moves to foot of stairs and calls upstairs:

TRACY. Is there a doctor in the house —?
CLIFF. (*off*) Who wants to know?!
TRACY. The doctor's chief cook-and-bottle-washer! Your breakfast is on the table! Get down here and eat it! You've got a big day ahead of you!
CLIFF. (*off*) You don't have to be so bossy!
TRACY. Today's my last chance! (*turns, moves toward front door*) May as well make the most of it! (*opens door, bends out of view slightly, straightens holding morning paper, and will cross room, glancing idly at front page,*

and lay the paper on the table handy to the place-setting; just as she arrives at table, CLIFF descends stairs into view, in elegant robe, slippers and pajamas; he looks slightly just-out-of-bed rumpled of hair, but is otherwise a reasonably attractive man in his mid-30s)

CLIFF. (*en route to table, where he will sit in* L. *chair)* What *time* is it, anyhow?

TRACY. I gather you didn't do much drinking at your bachelor party.

CLIFF. Why do you gather *that*?

TRACY. 'Cause you didn't ask me what *day* it was.

CLIFF. (*seated by now, buttering toast)* Doctors are health-conscious. I'm not sure there *was* any liquor at that party.

TRACY. Then where's your wristwatch?

CLIFF. (*stares blankly at bare wrist, gives a de-fuzzing shake of his head)* It'll come to me, it'll come to me. Meanwhile, what *time* is it?

TRACY. (*filling his coffeecup)* About eight-forty-five.

CLIFF. Oh. (*takes cup, starts to drink)*

TRACY. *Ay*-em.

CLIFF. (*scowls, sets down cup, starts eating)* I *knew* that, I *knew* that. Didn't have *that* much to drink last night . . . (*she stares at him, he gets slightly uneasy)* It *was* — uh — *last* night, right?

TRACY. Brother dearest, if you're hoping you've overslept right into your wedding day, no such luck. It's still twenty-four hours in the offing.

CLIFF. Twenty-seven. The wedding's not till noon.

TRACY. It's *still* coming up mighty quick, Cliff. Why couldn't Miss Ralston do the *traditional* thing and get married in *June*!

CLIFF. She's in love. She couldn't *wait* another six months. So why delay it?

TRACY. It'd give you a chance to meet somebody even *more* attractive, maybe.

CLIFF. (*sets down fork*) Trace . . . you—you don't *like* Bobbi very much, do you!

TRACY. (*abruptly contrite*) Oh . . . honestly, I don't actively *dis*like her . . . it's just—oh, never mind. (*turns, starts for* K.D.) None of my business, anyhow—!

CLIFF. Tracy. (*she stops, but doesn't turn around*) Come on, sis. Level with me. I'm getting *married* to a wonderful woman. You should be *happy* about it.

TRACY. (*still not turned*) Who says I'm *not?*

CLIFF. You always *hum* when you're happy.

TRACY. (*turns to face him*) I figured your hangover would appreciate the silence.

CLIFF. I don't *have* a hangover! (*his own shout makes him wince and finger his temples*) Much.

TRACY. Aw, Cliff, I'm sorry. It's just—well—you know—up until today, I've cooked your meals, cleaned your apartment, sent your suits to the cleaners—I guess I haven't quite adjusted to the notion of some *other* woman taking over my chores.

CLIFF. Tracy, are you nuts? Bobbi couldn't pick a cookbook out of a police lineup! And I don't think she's ever *seen* a dust rag—*or* the inside of a dry cleaner's shop.

TRACY. (*abruptly impassioned*) Then *why* are you—?! (*regains control*) You'd better eat your breakfast before it gets cold. (*turns toward* K.D. *again, but pauses on:*)

CLIFF. Trace. Sit down. Please. I want to talk to you.

TRACY. (*takes coffeecup from apron pocket, sits in* R. *chair, pours herself a cup of coffee, and is just bringing it to her lips when she sees his look*) I believe in being prepared. (*takes sip of coffee*)

CLIFF. I thought *I* planned this little discussion.

TRACY. Eat your breakfast.

CLIFF. (*obediently resumes doing so, almost like a guilty schoolboy*) All right, all right, I'm eating! (*stops piece of toast just short of mouth*) But *why* are you so gloomy about my upcoming marriage? Tell me. It's important to me. *You're* important to me.

TRACY. It's just — well — honestly, Cliff, what do you *see* in Bobbi Ralston?

CLIFF. (*sets toast on plate, ponders a moment; then:*) Well . . . first off, you've got to admit she's beautiful.

TRACY. Like an Estee Lauder spokeswoman.

CLIFF. And intelligent?

TRACY. Phi Beta Kappa from top to toe.

CLIFF. Good manners?

TRACY. She could oversee a foreign embassy.

CLIFF. Nice figure?

TRACY. She'd make your average centerfold look like Raggedy Ann.

CLIFF. Then *what* — ?

TRACY. Flat out?

CLIFF. Flat out.

TRACY. (*takes a breath; then:*) I just don't think *she* is particularly crazy about *you*!

CLIFF. *What*?!

TRACY. You have a hearing problem?

CLIFF. I hear quite clearly, thank you; I just can't believe what I heard. Tracy, if Bobbi didn't *love* me, why would she be *marrying* me tomorrow?

TRACY. (*drains cup, stands*) You're young, good-looking, very well off financially, *and* the most renowned plastic surgeon in the history of tummy-tucks and face-lifts, and could easily keep any wife of yours looking young and radiant into her sixties! That makes you the catch of the century, darling brother. No woman with half a brain would *dare* turn you down!

CLIFF. Are you saying Bobbi Ralston is marrying me because she likes *her* looks?!

TRACY. Are *you* imagining she's *not*? (*Exits with coffeecup via* K.D.)

CLIFF. (*pushes chair back, stands*) Tracy, are you nuts?! Bobbi and I are about the same age, have the same circle of friends, enjoy the same amusements, even drink the same brands of liquor! If that isn't bride-material, what *is* it?!

TRACY. (*steps back via* K.D. *minus coffeecup, stops; then:*) A fraternity brother.

CLIFF. A husband and wife *should* be friends!

TRACY. Look, if *friendship's* all you want, buy a dachshund!

CLIFF. (*blurts*) A *dachshund* can't endow a *clinic!* (*has said too much, instantly tries to cool down*) I — I didn't mean that the way it sounded.

TRACY. (*very gently*) A dachshund *can* endow a clinic — ?

CLIFF. (*slumps wearily*) Tracy. Do you know how many *millions* of dollars it takes to build a children's clinic? Bobbi serves on a dozen committees, knows all the "right people" to put the arm on for donations, is a whiz at masterminding charity drives —

TRACY. For the price of a small band of gold . . . ?

CLIFF. It's *not* small, and it happens to be *platinum!*

TRACY. (*uncontrite*) Forgive me.

CLIFF. Aw . . . aw, damn it! (*moves listlessly to sofa, sits on* D.S. *end, facing out front*) Trace . . . do you have any *idea* how cruel children can be? Think of a little kid, a kid with an oversized nose — or big ears — or a bad harelip — do you know how *nasty* his unfeeling young peers can be to him? He gets taunted, teased, mercilessly badgered — he ends up a real hate-case — not wanting to go to school, wishing he could *kill* his tormentors — and — worst of all — when he's alone — he *cries* a lot. (*looks over at her*) Kids have *enough* to cry about in life, even the good-looking ones. So what's so wrong about trying to *do* something for them, at a price even *poor* kids can afford?

TRACY. (*quietly*) I never said you shouldn't. I just think — hope — pray — that there's got to be a better way of *getting* that endowment.

CLIFF. Aw, hell, Trace . . . (*stands, shrugs lamely*) Bobbi's not so *bad*, really. We get along. She's pleasant company. And very easy on the eyes.

TRACY. But would you share her *toothbrush*?

CLIFF. Would I *what* — ?

TRACY. I read someplace that's the Test Of True Love.

CLIFF. Well, you're wrong. True Love is not caring if she *owns* a toothbrush! (*starts for stairs*) I've gotta get dressed. Bobbi's gonna *be* here at any moment! (*just as he reaches foot of stairs, door buzzer sounds*) Oh damn.

TRACY. (*crosses toward him*) Say, *I've* got a plan: Why not let her see you as you *normally* look in the morning: slightly unshaven, hair not quite combed, egg on your chin — (*he wipes hastily at chin as she reaches him and continues*) — and maybe she'll be so shocked she'll give you an endowment *not* to marry her! (*buzzer sounds again; she steps to door, turns head toward him*) Shall we let her in and find out?

CLIFF. Don't you *dare* open that door! (*starts up stairs*)

TRACY. You'd rather disillusion her *after* the wedding night — ?

CLIFF. (*stops, then starts downstairs again, slowly*)

Tracy, I'm gonna call your bluff! Go ahead, let her in! My appearance won't make the slightest bit of difference to her!

TRACY. (*hand goes to doorknob*) You're probably right. She'll be so busy giving you your living-instructions for the day that she won't even *notice* your decrepitude! (*BUZZER SOUNDS AGAIN, HOLDING A BIT LONGER; she starts to turn knob*)

CLIFF. Hold it! What was that crack about her giving me *instructions*?

TRACY. Are you saying Bobbi *doesn't* treat you like an errand-boy?

CLIFF. (*miffed*) Listen, kiddo, if she *did* try the strong-arm approach, I'd tell *her* a thing or two! I'm as non-chauvinistic as the next man, but I do *not* think a woman should push a man around!

TRACY. (*mock-soothing*) Now-now, it's not her fault. She's a dedicated anthropologist; she's used to giving orders to the digging-crew.

CLIFF. Well, she's *not* giving 'em to *me!*

TRACY. Not until I open the *door*, at least.

CLIFF. Okay, Miss Smartypants! *Open* the door! And just *one* push from Bobbi, and you'll see some fireworks! *I* know how to handle the situation!

(*BUZZER STARTS LONG AND UNINTERRUPTED BUZZING*)

TRACY. Fair enough. (*opens door immediately; buzzer stops, and BOBBI RALSTON surges into foyer; she is totally attractive, well-dressed in a fur coat and very stylish boots, carrying a large modish purse; she sights CLIFF and as if TRACY weren't even present she addresses him peremptorily:*)

BOBBI. Clifford, I nearly wore my *thumb* out pressing that button! Oh! You're not even dressed yet! You have to pick up your tuxedo at the rental place in fifteen minutes, and *then* I want you to see the florist about the bridal bouquet — it *froze* or something and has to be thawed, or maybe vice-versa — and you've got to get to the airport and pick up my mother at twelve-oh-five, and the moment you drop her at her hotel, get right over to the caterer's and make *sure* they're using *fresh* shrimp on the canapes — then *do* hurry over to Muffy Armbruster's prenuptial cocktail party, or whatever she's calling it, and I'll meet you there at three-thirty *sharp* as soon as I finish my last fitting, and don't forget to wear that dark maroon tie I picked out for you — oh, *and* those cufflinks Aunt Penny gave you at Christmas, because if she pops in at Muffy's she'll *expect* you to be wearing them, even if you *do* hate imitation emeralds, and then we can *dash* to Elmer and Faleen's for a quick dinner, and maybe manage to get there before all the *hors d'oeuvre* are gone! Ta-ta! (*Exits to hall, closing door behind her; there is an eloquent silence between TRACY and CLIFF for about three beats; then:*)

TRACY. I thought you handled that splendidly.

CLIFF. (*avoids her gaze, gallops upstairs on:*) Excuse me, I've got to dress!

TRACY. Don't forget to wear your track shoes!

CLIFF. (*off*) I can't. They clash with my stopwatch!

TRACY. (*laughs, starts down into living room, but stops as buzzer sounds*) That's strange. She can't *possibly* have left anything *out* . . . ?! (*returns to foyer and opens door; JAKE PUTNAM Enters, casual in slacks and windbreaker, carrying a briefcase*) Why, if it isn't Lawyer Putnam! Time to foreclose our mortgage?

JAKE. What mortgage? Cliff paid *cash* for this condo.

TRACY. (*will close door and follow him down into livingroom, where he's just tossing his briefcase onto lower end of sofa*) Well, you *are* dressed for a *casual* call, but when I saw your official briefcase—

JAKE. (*fingers briefly to temples*) There's no need to *shout!*

TRACY. Oh, that's right, *you* were at last night's bachelor bash, too! Can I get you something . . . aspirin . . . Alka-Seltzer—cyanide?

JAKE. It's all your *brother's* fault. He was having such a lousy time I had to drink for *two!*

TRACY. Well, the best man *is* supposed to keep things chugging along.

JAKE. Is the groom out from under the icebag yet?

TRACY. Actually, he's in better shape than I'd have expected. He's up, he's getting dressed, and if his eyes are bloodshot I must be getting colorblind.

JAKE. Are you saying Cliff came home *sober?*

TRACY. *Somber* is more like it. But Cliff only drinks when he's having a good time.

JAKE. Then he can save big on today's liquor bill: I have news.

TRACY. (*has passed him and is just starting to clear breakfast things, but pauses and turns to face him on:*) *Bad* news, Jake?

JAKE. Mmm, probably not really—*ill-timed* is more like it.

TRACY. Oh, good. I thought it might be a malpractice suit. (*will now clear breakfast things, piling cutlery onto plate, hefting coffeepot tray in one hand and plate in the other, etc., so she can clear and exit with things in one trip, during:*) I could just picture some high-society matron awakening to find her nose was where her *ear* used to be!

JAKE. Actually, my tidings might be *pleasant* if Cliff weren't about to plunge into holy matrimony tomorrow.

TRACY. (*off*) Don't tell me you've arrived with a stay of execution?

JAKE. You make it sound as if Cliff were standing on a banana peel before the jaws of doom! Why be so negative about it?

TRACY. (*off*) I was just taking my cue from Cliff. I've seen happier smiles on people heading for a root-canal! (*re-enters via* K.D.) Say, would you like a cup of coffee? That's no way to be dressed in New York City in January! [*NOTE: Lighting outside window will start to change at this point, almost imperceptibly, from bright and cheery to gloomy and gray, with an every-so-often light sprinkling of snowflakes outside the pane; the entire transition should take about five minutes.*]

JAKE. (*has picked up paper from table, is glancing idly at front page*) I parked in the basement garage. I hate driving in an overcoat.

TRACY. Try to get a simple answer from a lawyer! Do you want coffee or don't you?

JAKE. (*looks up from paper*) Maybe I could use a cup at that. (*will sit at* L. *end of table during:*) Your elevator sits in the basement so long, it was like riding up in a refrigerator. (*will page idly through paper as TRACY Exits to kitchen*)

TRACY. (*off*) So look, if you're *not* here with a stay of execution, what *are* you here with?

JAKE. (*still reading*) A bequest. Or, to be accurate, *news* of a bequest. The bequest itself should be here at any moment.

TRACY. (*will re-enter with cup of coffee, during:*) Oh, *now* I see what you meant, before. Poor Cliff. He'll be terribly upset.

JAKE. (*drops paper, takes cup, starts sipping*) Upset about what, getting a bequest?

TRACY. No-no, I just meant that a bequest always means somebody has *died*, and that's awfully upsetting news just before his wedding—it's upsetting news *any* time. Who died?

JAKE. James Lomax Fesco of Cleveland, Ohio.

TRACY. *I* don't know any James Lomax Fesco.

JAKE. No reason you *should.* Cliff didn't know him, either.

TRACY. How's that again—?

JAKE. Under the law, Tracy, a person making out his will can leave any*thing* they want to any*body* they want, whether they know the lucky winner or not.

TRACY. (*will take cup as JAKE rises from chair*) But why leave something to somebody you don't even know? (*Exits via* K.D.)

JAKE. People leave things to *institutions*—churches, museums, like that—(*shrugs*) Why not to other *people*?

TRACY. (*re-entering minus cup*) But—to a total *stranger*?

JAKE. (*will stroll up behind bar, pour himself a brandy, during:*) Ah, but the illustrious Doctor Clifford Tucker is *not* a stranger. He's world-famous, Tracy, like a politician or a gangster or a movie star. Cliff may not have known Mister Fesco, but Mister Fesco couldn't *help* but know *him!* (*abruptly, sets brandy down on end of bar, moves* U.R.) Excuse me a minute—the cold weather and that coffee are *getting* to me. Be right back. Unless your personal bathroom isn't fit to be seen at the moment—?

TRACY. It's just fine. But please don't look at the *bed!*

JAKE. Why, who's in it?

TRACY. Listen, when *I* finally land Prince Charming, I'll send out formal announcements!

JAKE. (*nods, almost completes exit, then stops and turns to her*) Seriously — how do you ever hope to *meet* Prince Charming cooped up in your brother's condominium? When was the last time you went out on the town and made whoopee?

TRACY. None of your damn business. Now *scoot*, before you have an accident! (*JAKE shrugs, but Exits* U.R.; *ever the domestic, TRACY moves behind bar, recaps the brandy bottle JAKE had left open there, and places it back on the liquor shelf where it belongs, then takes a cocktail napkin from behind bar someplace, lifts his brandy glass, and puts napkin under it, calling after him — whether he can hear her or not:*) A girl gets awfully tired of going out *scouting* for a man. I figure if I wait long enough, some day my prince will simply show up at our front door, suitcase in hand, and carry me off to happyland — if I'm not wearing curlers at the time!

JAKE. (far *off*) *What* — ?

TRACY. (*calls*) Nothing important! . . . Oh, by the way, just how much *is* this bequest? I don't suppose it's enough to endow a *clinic* . . . ? If it *is*, I might just exhume James Lomax Fesco and kiss his icy little forehead!

JAKE. (*off, but louder*) Kiss his *what*? I can't hear you with the bathroom door closed!

TRACY. Then leave it open another second and tell me how much *cash* Lomax left us!

JAKE. (*still off*) Oh, he didn't leave *money*!

TRACY. Then what *did* he leave?

JAKE. (*off*) *His only child*! (*as TRACY gapes, we hear JAKE shut the bathroom door, simultaneous with:*)

TRACY. His *WHAT*?! (*she moves as if to exit after JAKE, but stops as CLIFF — now dressed in suit and tie — trots downstairs, mumbling to himself en route:*)

CLIFF. Tuxedo, bouquet, airport, hotel, caterer—(*stops, frowns, turns toward TRACY*) *Why* am I going to the caterer's—?

TRACY. *Fresh* shrimp on the canapes.

CLIFF. (*relieved*) Ah, right! (*moves past her toward* K.R., *via which he will exit while continuing:*) Let's see now . . . caterer, then Muffy's cocktail party, and—

TRACY. (*will move* D.S. *slightly to see out via* K.R. *into kitchen*) You're not wearing that maroon tie. *Or* Aunt Penny's cufflinks!

CLIFF. (*off*) The maroon tie is spotted with sushi, and those cufflinks look like something Aunt Penny carved out of an old *Coke* bottle!

TRACY. She *said* those imitation emeralds were *imported*!

CLIFF. (*off*) Okay, then, an old *Beck's* bottle! (*will re-enter via* K.R., *sipping a glass of milk, during:*) How much time do I have left?

TRACY. (*amused*) *Still* haven't found your wristwatch, have you!

CLIFF. Please. How . . . much . . . time?!

TRACY. As a carefree bachelor?

CLIFF. To get to the *tux*-rental shop! (*takes a long drink of milk*)

TRACY. Shall I order some more cases of Maalox?

CLIFF. What for?

TRACY. You hate milk. The only time you drink it is when your ulcer starts kicking up.

CLIFF. It was only a twinge. I'll be fine, just fine. (*sets emptied glass on end of bar, suddenly spots briefcase on sofa*) Whose briefcase is that?

TRACY. Your loyal little lawyer's. (*reacts to own alliteration*) *Boy*, that's hard to say!

CLIFF. Jake? Here? Today?

Tracy. Yes. Yes. Yes.

Cliff. But what for? I mean, Bobbi and I already *signed* that prenuptial thing.

Tracy. I hate prenuptial agreements. They're like planning the divorce in advance.

Cliff. A couple should be *prudent.* (*JAKE will re-enter* u.r. *during:*) What happens if all that hot blood cools down?

Jake. Especially at the South Pole.

Cliff. Oh, hi, Jake.

Tracy. What's all this about the South Pole?

Jake. That's where Cliff and Bobbi are honeymooning. You didn't *know*?

Tracy. Who'd even *suspect*?! Cliff, tell me he's kidding.

Cliff. Now-now, sis, it'll be perfectly fine. It's mid-*summer* down there now.

Tracy. Then why haven't you packed your suntan oil?

Cliff. Okay, so it's a bit on the chilly side. We're taking plenty of warm clothing.

Tracy. I can't be hearing right. You really *are* honeymooning at the South Pole? *Why*?

Cliff. Well, for one thing, we know we won't be *disturbed* . . . besides, it'll give my anthropologist bride the chance to test some of her theories.

Tracy. "Two can freeze as cheaply as one"?

Jake. It's Bobbi's golden opportunity to disprove Darwin's theory about the origins of mankind. *She* thinks the human race descended from *penguins*.

Cliff. (*starts toward foyer*) Can we discuss this some other time? I've got to go get a *tux*!

Tracy. Gee, maybe Bobbi's theory is *right*!

CLIFF. (*stops*) Look, *anyone* can honeymoon at Niagara Falls or Acapulco or Tahiti—!

JAKE. Anyone but Clifford Tucker.

CLIFF. Listen, *I* can honeymoon anywhere I want to!

TRACY. The South Pole was *your* idea?

CLIFF. (*fumes, but starts toward foyer again, where he will get his overcoat off the rack there, during:*) I *don't* see why a loving couple can't conduct a little *research* just because they happen to be newlyweds!

TRACY. *I* see — *she* can go poking among the penguins while *you* check out plastic surgery for chilblains!

CLIFF. (*donning overcoat*) I don't have time to discuss it now!

JAKE. Do you have half a moment for a little *legal* matter?

CLIFF. Is *that* why you're here?

JAKE. I didn't come to measure you for *snowshoes*.

CLIFF. (*buttoning coat, steps down into room again, curious*) Then why *are* you here, Jake?

TRACY. You have a surprise wedding present from Cleveland.

CLIFF. That it takes a *lawyer* to deliver? What *kind* of present?

TRACY. (*takes his milk glass, will exit* K.R. *with it during:*) Jake will fill you in. Just promise me *I* can be in the room when you tell your *bride*!

CLIFF. Jake, what is she talking about? And *hurry*, I have a million things to do.

JAKE. James Lomax Fesco of Cleveland, Ohio, has died and left you his only child.

CLIFF. His *what*?! I didn't even *know* the man!

JAKE. Her name is Annabel. She'll be arriving here at any moment.

CLIFF. But how *can* she? I mean, people can't leave their kids to *strangers*?!

JAKE. Oh, yes they can.

TRACY. (*re-entering via K.R. minus milk glass*) I wish *our* parents knew about laws like that! I might've talked them into leaving *me* to *Robert Redford*!

CLIFF. Look, this is all some silly mistake. *You* handle it for me, Jake. You know every legal loophole in the history of jurisprudence. Now, if you'll excuse me — (*looks at bare wrist, makes annoyed face*) What *time* is it, anyhow?!

JAKE. *Oh*! That reminds me — (*takes wristwatch from pocket, hands it to CLIFF*) You forgot this last night.

CLIFF. (*slipping it onto wrist*) Thank heaven! This Rolex is a gift from Bobbi! Where did I leave it?

JAKE. Snugly looped around Miss Vavoom's left ankle!

TRACY. What was this *Miss Vavoom* doing at your bachelor party? Or shouldn't I pry?

CLIFF. (*brushing at watchband*) What's this sticky white stuff?

JAKE. Cake frosting.

TRACY. I think *that* answers my question.

CLIFF. Look, I've really got to run. Jake, when they trot the tiny tot around, simply explain to them that I don't *want* the kid, and have them take it to somebody else.

TRACY. Shouldn't you talk it over with *Bobbi* first? Or don't you *want* that clinic?

CLIFF. What's Annabel Fesco got to do with the *clinic*?

TRACY. Doesn't it depend on Bobbi getting donations from all those "right people," pleading your noble cause, and assuring them you're *worthy* of all that cash?

CLIFF. Well, sure, of course it does, but what's that got to do with Annabel Fesco?

TRACY. (*to JAKE*) Shall *I* tell him, or will *you*?

JAKE. Allow *me*! Cliff, I'm your attorney, not your publicist, but won't your public image turn just a *teensy* bit sour if the world learns you ignore the wishes of the dying and throw orphans out in the snow?

CLIFF. (*absorbs this for one wide-eyed moment; then:*) Yipe.

TRACY. (*after a short pause*) Look, why don't *I* go pick up that tux, and do the bit with the caterer and all? You two have things to talk about.

CLIFF. But you don't drive, Trace.

TRACY. There's always the subway.

CLIFF. It doesn't stop at Kennedy Airport. Bobbi's *mother* is arriving, and—Look, Jake, work *something* out, please, will you? I've really got to get *out* of here!

JAKE. But Cliff, there's only so *much* a lawyer can do—!

CLIFF. (*moves to foyer and opens door*) I can poke a *few* holes in my itinerary—after I stash Mrs. Ralston at her hotel, I can *stiff* Muffy's cocktail party and rush right back, okay? I just can't tackle the Cleveland Orphan situation *now*! (*Exits, shutting door after him*)

JAKE. *That* was kind of callous, even for a nervous groom . . .

TRACY. He'll be back. It just hasn't had a chance to sink in yet. With that list of things *Bobbi* laid on him, it's a wonder he remembered to put on his *overcoat*!

JAKE. (*moves to bar and retrieves his brandy glass*) She *is* a bossy little thing, isn't she! Go here, go there, do this, do that! (*takes stiff swallow of brandy*) How could a normal sane human male fall in love with a woman like *that*?!

TRACY. (*after a pause*) How *did* you?

JAKE. (*about to drink again, stops, lowers glass*) I didn't know it showed. (*moves slowly toward sofa*)

Tracy — what am I going to do? It's going to put a hell of a strain on the lawyer-client relationship. (*sits on* D. *end of sofa, nursing drink*) I'll be in agony, probably irritable, or at least stand-offish, and the poor guy won't even know *why*! Maybe I should tender my resignation right now.

TRACY. *That'd* be a lovely wedding present!

JAKE. (*comes to his feet*) Damn! Do you know — I haven't even *gotten* her a present yet!

TRACY. (*gently*) Gotten *them* a present yet.

JAKE. (*laughs ruefully*) Maybe *that's* why I haven't. No matter what I get her, it'll be shared with *Cliff,* instead of with *me,* and I'm — I'm just not up to it, Tracy. Feeling the way I do, what kind of wedding gift could I *get* for the two of them, anyhow?!

TRACY. How about twin beds?

JAKE. (*this unexpected reply shatters his gloom, and he bursts into laughter — slightly rueful laughter — almost tearful; then he manages to gasp:*) Oh, Tracy! . . . Oh, that's marvelous! . . . Thank you. I really needed that.

TRACY. Had to say *something* — (*gestures toward window, where the view is now grim and snowy*) — your mood was grayer than today's *weather*! Jake, why don't you *tell* her?

JAKE. What would it accomplish? She'd *still* go ahead and marry Cliff, and things would be so awkward afterward that he'd just about *have* to ask me to resign!

TRACY. But what if she *didn't* go ahead and marry Cliff? She might just *like* you, you know.

JAKE. With all the wedding arrangements made, and her mother arriving, and the invitations out, and the church booked — that's too much social pressure. The wedding's a shoo-in. At *this* stage, it's too hard *not* to go through with things, *whatever* second thoughts Bobbi might have. And then *she'd* be miserable, and *I'd* be miserable, and—hell, I can't do that to her!

TRACY. You'd rather remain undeclared, and spend the rest of your life *wondering* what might have happened if you spoke up?

JAKE. If I thought for one single moment that I had the slightest *chance* of—Aw, hell, why kid myself! (*drains glass, starts for bar*) I need another brandy!

TRACY. (*moves behind bar as he arrives, gets brandy bottle*) Let me do the honors. You men always make such a mess! (*as she pours him a fresh brandy, puts the bottle back, etc.:*)

JAKE. I sure hope Bobbi can keep house half as well as you do, for Cliff's sake. Come to think of it, what *is* the upcoming arrangement? Do you stay on to take care of *both* of them, now—or do you tend to Cliff and let Bobbi fend for herself?

TRACY. (*hesitates, then says without emotion:*) They won't be living here. He'll be moving into Bobbi's apartment after their return.

JAKE. You'll be living here all by yourself? *There's* a gloomy prospect! (*takes brandy from her, starts to sip at it*)

TRACY. (*avoiding his gaze*) I'll be just fine. I don't need a place this big. I'll find one of my own. I can't spend *all* my life living on my brother's charity. (*heads for* K.R.) Excuse me, I have dishes to do.

JAKE. But how will you *support* yourself? You've devoted so much of your life to taking care of your brother —do you *have* any job-skills other than domestic ones?

TRACY. (*stops short of* K.R. *exit*) I'm not sure. I can type a little—filing's not so hard. I just hope I don't have to have any *computer*-skills; I can't even program our new *answering*-machine! (*points toward phone-table*) I get nervous around machinery that thinks for itself.

JAKE. You know, *you* sound about as happy over the upcoming nuptials as *I* do!

TRACY. That's nonsense. I hope Cliff and Bobbi will be *very* happy.

JAKE. Then why aren't you *humming*?

TRACY. I'm saving my vocal cords for whenever Prince Charming decides to show up. Now, let's *drop* the topic, okay? I have work to do.

JAKE. That reminds me—where are you going to stash Orphan Annie when she arrives?

TRACY. *Who*? . . . Oh, you mean little Annabel? Actually, I haven't given it much thought. I suppose the kid can share *my* room for awhile—kids don't take up much space.

JAKE. But will *Bobbi* cotton to the notion of having a child on the premises? I mean, after the honeymoon, Annabel belongs wherever *Cliff* will be residing.

TRACY. Damn. That *is* a problem. But it's not *my* problem. I'll lay it on Cliff.

JAKE. *If* he ever comes *back*! He was starting to turn *green* at the Cleveland-bequest situation. No *wonder* he skedaddled out of here.

TRACY. I have a feeling his conscience will bring him back, soon as matters really sink in. He just has a lot on his mind today, what with the wedding and all. (*then both look* U.L. *as CLIFF storms into foyer*) There, what'd I tell you! Cliff always was a softy where *kids* are concerned.

CLIFF. This has nothing to do with Ohio orphans! The stupid *car* won't start! Frozen fuel line!

JAKE. I'm not surprised. You'd think a building this expensive could afford a *heated* garage.

TRACY. I've been after him for years to relocate in southern California.

CLIFF. For what? I hate to drive, I can't swim, and I sunburn!

TRACY. Hire a chauffeur, get fitted for waterwings, and buy a beach umbrella.

CLIFF. You just want to meet movie stars.

TRACY. Is that a crime?

CLIFF. Look, I laid out almost half a million bucks for this condo, the least I can do is *live* in it!

JAKE. Would you like to borrow *my* car, Cliff? I only just parked it — the fuel line can't have frozen *yet.*

CLIFF. Hey, that would be great! . . . Oh, wait, I can't drive a stick-shift. But if I don't pick up that tux and get Bobbi's mother at the airport — !

JAKE. (*drains brandy glass, leaves it on bar, heads for sofa*) Help is on the way, *mon capitan!* (*grabs up brief-case, starts for door*) I'll *drive* you!

CLIFF. It's a hell of an imposition, Jake —

JAKE. What are best friends for? Get moving, will you?!

CLIFF. (*heads for door*) Right! And thanks! (*as he Exits to hall, with JAKE just a pace behind him:*)

TRACY. If you run out of gas in a lonely spot — I'll understand.

JAKE. I just filled the tank this morning, damn it. But thanks for the thought! (*grins at her, then Exits, shutting door after him; TRACY picks up his empty glass, starts with it for* K.R., *stops as phone rings, wavers, then sets glass back onto bar and answers phone*)

TRACY. Hello? . . . *What* advertisement? . . . No, it must be a misprint . . . Look, I'm sorry, but take my word for it, Doctor Tucker does *not* need a roommate to share the rent! (*hangs up, barely turns for glass on bar when phone rings again; gets it*) Hello? . . . No, I'm sorry, that's a printing error or something . . . I don't *care* what the Village Voice says, they've listed the wrong telephone number! . . . No. Scout's honor, we do not *need* a roommate, do not *want* a roommate, or have any *use* for a roommate! (*hangs up; door buzzer sounds; she grimaces but stolidly answers it; LANGDON BAR-NETT, about 30, eager-looking and pleasant of aspect, pops in; he wears boots, jeans, flannel shirt, open canvas jacket, and carries a hefty suitcase in his right hand, a copy of the* Village Voice *in his left; TRACY takes a slight backstep, staring at him, on:*)

LANGDON. Is this the place that advertised for a roommate?

TRACY. (*looks him up and down; then:*) Yes it is! (*gestures into living room*) Come right in! (*as he Enters, phone rings again; she frowns, shuts door, starts for phone, then stops and queries hopefully:*) Do you know how to program an answering machine?

LANGDON. (*sets suitcase* R. *of sofa, drops newspaper on top of it*) Why, sure, ma'am. (*starts for phone* [*which will ring at normal intervals during dialogue*]) Can't you?

TRACY. (*following him across room*) I could the *old* one, but Doctor Tucker got this fancy new all-in-one microchip edition, and it's got so many buttons I'm afraid to touch it.

LANGDON. (*picks up phone* [*ringing stops*]; *speaks into phone*) Just a moment, please. (*presses button, turns to TRACY*) I have them on "Hold"; now what?

TRACY. Put a message on there that'll make them stop calling about sharing the rent.

LANGDON. Easy as pie. (*pushes button, then another, then speaks into phone*) Hi, there! I'm sorry to tell you that Doctor Tucker already *has* a new roommate! Better luck next time! (*pushes another button, hangs up*) There. That should hold them off for awhile, Miss—uh—?

TRACY. "Tracy."

LANGDON. Miss Tracy.

TRACY. No-no, it's Miss *Tucker*. My *first* name is "Tracy." What's *your* name?

LANGDON. Uh. Let me think . . . "Barnett . . . Langdon Barnett!"

TRACY. You don't sound very *sure* about it.

LANGDON. I'm not used to it yet. It's my stage name.

TRACY. Oh, you're an actor?

LANGDON. Trying to be. I'm studying at the American Theatre Wing.

TRACY. And they won't take you without a stage name?

LANGDON. No, the stage name was my *own* idea. Couldn't have my *right* name on a marquee.

TRACY. Now, that's just plain silly. *Everybody* uses real names in theatre nowadays—Jo Ann Pflug—Carrie Snodgress—Meryl Streep. Why go for an alias?

LANGDON. If I used my *real* name, people would laugh at me.

TRACY. Nonsense. It can't possibly be that bad. What *is* it?

LANGDON. (*hesitates: then:*) Lionel Barrymore.

TRACY. (*after a pause*) I see what you mean. Well, now, Langdon—or do you prefer "Lionel"—?

LANGDON. "Langdon," please. It'll help me get used to it.

TRACY. Would you like a brandy?

LANGDON. *Would* I! . . . I mean, yes, thanks, I really would. It's *cold* out there!

TRACY. (*gestures him toward sofa as she heads behind bar to pour him a drink*) That's what I figured. Sit down and relax while I get it. (*hums happily*)

LANGDON. (*sits a bit hesitantly*) Don't you want to discuss my financial condition? . . . references? . . . character?

TRACY. Later, later. First thing, we've got to heat you up—*warm* you up. (*will take glass of brandy and start toward sofa with it*) Then we can discuss your qualifications.

LANGDON. This—uh—Doctor Tucker—he's your father—? (*she arrives with brandy; he takes it gratefully*) Thank you! (*sips at it eagerly as she responds:*)

TRACY. My brother. I keep house for him.

LANGDON. (*looks about, admiringly*) You do a nice job of it, Miss Tucker.

TRACY. "Tracy," please. I mean, if we're going to be *living* together—

LANGDON. (*comes to his feet, wide-eyed*) You mean—I've *got* it?! The room, the rent-sharing? Just like that?

TRACY. Why are you so surprised?

LANGDON. Well, for one thing, that message you had me put on your machine! Naturally, I figured it meant you'd *found* a roommate . . .

TRACY. And I have. You're it.

LANGDON. But you don't know anything *about* me—you don't even know if I can *afford* to share the rent on this place . . . and, by the looks of this place, I probably *can't!*

TRACY. Did I so much as *mention* money?

LANGDON. No. You didn't. That's what scares me.

TRACY. *Scares* you?

LANGDON. You know—the guy meets a girl, she offers him a drink, the scene fades out, and when it fades back in, he's in an alley with all his money gone, or his ship has sailed without him, or he's got amnesia and can't remember why he's holding a gory dagger over the body of a man he doesn't even know, or—

TRACY. (*gently presses him back onto sofa*) Whoa, boy! You see too many movies! Come to think of it, how does an aspiring actor *manage* to get to the movies? They're not cheap, these days.

LANGDON. I have a late-night job after classes as a short-order cook. It's not a real classy place, but I can make a hell of a cheeseburger.

TRACY. Well, that puts you one-up on my *brother*! I don't think he can boil water! Which reminds me—he's leaving for the South Pole tomorrow, and you're *just* what I need to fill the gap.

LANGDON. (*uneasy, starts to get up*) You mean, I'd be sharing this apartment with *you*? . . . *Alone* with you?

TRACY. (*this time* shoves *him back down*) Don't be so *jumpy*! I thought struggling actors shared with *anybody*!

LANGDON. Well, maybe if—Look, how soon will your brother be coming back?

TRACY. He won't be *coming* back.

LANGDON. (*pops to his feet*) You know, maybe I *will* be going, now—!

TRACY. Will you get your mind off *murder*-plots?! He's going to the South Pole to *honeymoon*!

LANGDON. Who's he marrying, an *eskimo*?

TRACY. You're thinking of the *other* pole. Nothing where he's going but penguins.

LANGDON. He's marrying a *penguin*?

TRACY. (*pushes him down onto sofa again*) He's marrying a lady anthropologist. Penguins are her life.

LANGDON. Then what does she want with your *brother*?

TRACY. Actually, that's what we're *all* puzzled about. But the point is, after seventeen years, I won't have anybody to *do* for, do you see? And it's gotten to be a kind of habit, tending to a man's needs, and when you showed up at the door, all at once I realized I wouldn't *have* to move out of this big apartment, and—
LANGDON. But *I* just wanted a place to *sleep* nights. I wasn't figuring on having a built-in *housekeeper!*
TRACY. So count your blessings!

(Then both look doorward as CLIFF and JAKE re-enter, CLIFF moving to hang his outerwear on rack while JAKE shuts door and heads to bar to refill his abandoned brandy glass, during:)

CLIFF. Now *his* car won't start!
JAKE. That garage is colder than I thought!
CLIFF. (*moving from coat rack toward phone*) Maybe that tux rental place *delivers!*
JAKE. You may have to get married in your workclothes if it doesn't!
TRACY. That'd be real togetherness—Bobbi in her veil, Cliff in his surgical mask . . .
CLIFF. (*putting phone to ear before dialing*) Don't forget Orphan Annie in her stroller!
TRACY. Ah! Then you've come around?
CLIFF. Hell, why not! It's no fun being an orphan. I oughta know! (*scowls, jiggles phone-receiver*)
TRACY. (*to LANGDON:*) My brother was adopted.
LANGDON. Oh.
JAKE. I sure hope that *social worker's* gas-line doesn't freeze up!
TRACY. *What* social worker?
CLIFF. You can't expect Annabel to find the way here

by *herself!* (*taps cradle-button again, rapidly, scowls, hangs up*) Damn! I think the *phone*-lines are frozen, too! (*moves toward stairs*) I'll try the upstairs extension.

TRACY. You may as well call the caterer and the florist, too, while you're at it. Time is starting to run out fast!

CLIFF. (*en route upstairs*) But what about Bobbi's *mother?* I can't pick *her* up by telephone!

TRACY. (*to LANGDON:*) Bobbi is Cliff's fiancee.

LANGDON. Oh.

JAKE. (*comes from behind bar with glass of brandy, stops CLIFF's ascent with:*) I'm sure Bobbi will be understanding once you explain.

TRACY. If he can get a *word* in!

CLIFF. She's *got* to pause for breath *sometime!* Hey, speaking of my Daily Chores, there's a *gap* in my mental list. I mean, there's Muffy's, the tux, the caterer, the florist, Bobbi's mother — and *what?*

TRACY. Your track shoes?

CLIFF. Seriously.

TRACY. Ah! Elmer and Faleen's for dinner! Though how you think you're driving all the way up to Scarsdale in this blizzard with a frozen fuel-line — !

JAKE. — *and* getting *back* here in time for that meet-Mrs.-Ralston party so Bobbi's mother can give you the onceover — !

TRACY. Listen, why don't you phone the airport and ask Mrs. Ralston to take a *cab* to her hotel or Bobbi's place?

CLIFF. At New York City cab-rates — ?!

JAKE. Rebecca Ralston is loaded. She can afford it.

CLIFF. But she's not going to *like* it! Damn! (*starts upstairs again*) The way things are going, I may have to telephone my *wedding*-responses tomorrow! (*ascends from view*)

TRACY. Jake, is that legal?

JAKE. Sometimes under very special circumstances.

TRACY. Well, you ought to know!

LANGDON. Why?

TRACY. Jake is Cliff's lawyer.

LANGDON. Oh.

JAKE. Hope he doesn't take too long. I've got to phone the motor club about my car.

TRACY. You mean you *really* couldn't get it started?

JAKE. Tracy, I may be a member of the bar, but I still have *some* integrity.

CLIFF. (*appears at top of stairs*) Tracy, may I ask you something?

TRACY. Of course. What would you like to know?

CLIFF. (*points at LANGDON*) Who the hell is *that*?

TRACY. Would you believe Lionel Barrymore?

LANGDON. Of course, I don't use my real name.

JAKE. (*fascinated*) What *is* your real name?

LANGDON. Lionel Barrymore.

JAKE. (*looks at brandy glass*) I think I've had enough of these.

CLIFF. Tracy, will you stop playing games and tell me who this guy is?

TRACY. My new roommate.

CLIFF. Since *when*?!

TRACY. Since you decided to move in with Bobbi.

CLIFF. You didn't consult *me* about him!

TRACY. You didn't consult *me* about *Bobbi*!

CLIFF. (*will descend stairs now, and Enter living room, during:*) Don't get cute! This is serious! As your brother, I demand an explanation!

TRACY. Fair enough. I figured it's going to be mighty *lonely* around here when you go off romping with the penguins, and it's a shame to let such a nice big bedroom go to waste, and it's kind of *nice* to have a man to take care of—

CLIFF. But who *is* he? Where did he *come* from? Why is he here *today*?

TRACY. His name is Lionel Barrymore, but he's an actor, so he changed it to Langdon Barnett—

LANGDON. I didn't want to change the initials. I have a monogrammed hairbrush.

CLIFF. Get it. I may want to use it on my sister!

TRACY. Cliff, be reasonable. He needs a place to stay, we *have* a place for him to stay—

LANGDON. Though you didn't mention how much my share is.

JAKE. Share of what?

LANGDON. The rent.

CLIFF. What are you talking about? There's no rent to *share*!

LANGDON. Gee, that's mighty generous of you, Doctor Tucker—

TRACY. He means he doesn't *pay* rent, Langdon. This is a condo.

LANGDON. How much is *that* likely to cost me?

TRACY. Nothing. Be my guest.

CLIFF. Tracy—!

TRACY. So sue me.

CLIFF. Jake—?

JAKE. Tracy, consider yourself sued.

LANGDON. I didn't mean to cause any trouble—

TRACY. And you didn't. Sit down and relax. When Cliff leaves, this place is mine to do with as I see fit.

CLIFF. But *until* I leave, this is *my* place, and I will *not* allow my sister to cohabitate with Lionel Barrymore!

TRACY. Clifford, dear, you're not *going* to leave if you don't make those *phone* calls!

CLIFF. Damn! I *forgot* about them! (*heads for stairs again*) We will *continue* this discussion the moment I return! (*as he races upstairs and vanishes:*)

JAKE. (*drains glass, sets it on bar*) I think the *brandy* is getting to me, now! Can I use your bathroom?

TRACY. Again?

JAKE. (*heading* U.R.) If the *pipes* haven't frozen! (*Exits*)

LANGDON. Listen, Miss Tucker—

TRACY. "Tracy."

LANGDON. Tracy. If my being here is going to get you into some kind of *trouble*—

TRACY. (*laughs*) Don't worry about it! Cliff's really very nice when he's not up to his ears in premarital jitters. (*door buzzer sounds*) Oh, maybe that's the social worker with Cliff's new daughter.

LANGDON. (*as she heads for door:*) Your brother's getting married tomorrow and he already has a daughter? Or mustn't I pry?

TRACY. (*pauses*) I mean she's new to *us*, I didn't mean he already has *another* daughter. Actually, she's an inheritance, but I figured "daughter" was the likeliest thing to call her. I mean — (*starts for door again*) — he already *has* a *sister*!

LANGDON. I don't quite understand *any* of this.

TRACY. (*at door*) Have another brandy. That should help.

LANGDON. (*sincerely*) Thanks!

(*As he heads for bar, where he'll replenish his glass, TRACY opens front door to admit ANNABEL FESCO, a ravishing young woman in her late 20s, wearing an overcoat and carrying a baby wrapped in a blanket.*)

TRACY. Ah! We were *expecting* you! Come in, come in! (*points at baby*) Annabel Fesco, right?

ANNABEL. Well, yes, but you see—

TRACY. Oh, what am I doing standing here! You must be absolutely *frozen*! Come in! (*business of shutting door, ushering ANNABEL into living room, during:*) Did you just come from the airport?

ANNABEL. From my hotel, actually. I wanted to freshen up before—

TRACY. How in the world did you find a *cab* in this weather?

ANNABEL. Oh, I walked. It's only five or six blocks—

TRACY. *Walked*?! You really *must* be frozen! And the *baby*, besides! I can offer *you* a brandy—(*to LANGDON, who's just finished pouring his fresh drink*) Langdon, will you get her a glass, please?

LANGDON. Sure thing! (*but his line practically over-laps hers as she continues her own earlier interrupted line:*)

TRACY. —but what in the world does one offer to a freezing *baby*?

ANNABEL. Oh, but you really needn't bother, because—

TRACY. Hot milk! Just the ticket! I'll get it right away! (*starts for* K.D.) Did you bring a bottle someplace? She looks too small to drink from a cup!

ANNABEL. (*forced to drop propriety:*) *Wait!* (*when a startled TRACY turns her way:*) There's no need! This *isn't* a baby!

TRACY. (*blankly*) Annabel isn't a baby? What *is* she —a *midget*?

ANNABEL. (*laughs*) No-no, *please* let me explain. You've been so kind and solicitous I haven't been able to get a *word* in! For starters, *I* am Annabel Fesco!

TRACY. My brother inherited *you*?!

LANGDON. (*coming from bar with ANNABEL's drink and his own*) Talk about *lucky*!

ANNABEL. Listen, it's very simple, if you'll let me go uninterrupted for a moment—(*pauses as LANGDON extends glass, takes it on:*) Thank you! (*takes sip, shivers slightly, then smiles*) Wow, that's really good stuff! I was chillier than I thought.

TRACY. Oh, my goodness, I never even took your coat. Here, let me—! (*will remove ANNABEL's overcoat and take it to coat rack, during:*) But I thought you *said* that baby-or-whatever-it-is *was* Annabel Fesco?

ANNABEL. That's because that's what my late father *named* it! It's a doll. His own very special invention. Looks like a real baby, feels like a real baby, even moves and makes noises like a real baby, and it doesn't take any batteries to function.

LANGDON. No kidding! But what powers it?

ANNABEL. A kind of one-way flywheel inside—you know, the same thing that powers a self-winding wristwatch. As long as the child keeps playing with her, she stores up enough energy to keep acting like a baby for hours and hours. (*"baby" suddenly starts to cry*) There, see what I mean!

TRACY. (*returning from rack*) What made her start doing that?

ANNABEL. A kind of *timer* inside. My father was quite ingenious. (*starts rocking "baby" in her arms*) There-there, Annabel, there-there . . . (*"baby" falls silent*) A couple of slow rocks and the mechanism turns right off again, see?

TRACY. But that's marvelous! A doll like that would be worth—probably *millions*!

ANNABEL. By any *other* name it would. The trouble is, the toy companies didn't think the name "Annabel Fesco" had enough class, and Dad kept insisting on it, because it was named after *me*, and—well—he still hadn't sold it when he died.

LANGDON. Those stinkers!

ANNABEL. My opinion exactly! But that's why Dad left it to Doctor Tucker, do you see?

TRACY. No, but let's sit *down* while you explain, I've been on my feet all day! (*to LANGDON:*) Put that *suitcase* somewhere, will you, before someone trips over it? (*LANGDON will stash suitcase and newspaper against wall* U.S. *of fireplace, while TRACY and ANNABEL sit on sofa together*) Now, what's this incredible invention got to do with my brother?

ANNABEL. Your brother is Doctor Tucker, right?

TRACY. Yes. Oh, and I'm being stupid—my name is Tracy, and this is Langdon Barnett—unless he changes his mind.

ANNABEL. How's that again?

LANGDON. I'm an actor. It's my stage name. See, my *real* name is—(*by now, he's sort of lounging back against* U. *end of fireplace*)

TRACY. Not *now*, Langdon. First I want to hear about this *inheritance* of Cliff's.

ANNABEL. Well, Dad had read about your brother in the papers for years, learned all about his wonderful devotion to children, and he told me he couldn't think of a *better* person to demonstrate "Annabel, Junior" to the world. With *his* endorsement, no one would *mind* what the doll was called, and he'd be able to make *so* many children happier all over the world with this new doll, and—

TRACY. And so he left it to my brother! What a *nice* nice person he must have been!

ANNABEL. He really was. And downright *obsessed*

with making *children* happy! That's why he decided your brother was the ideal person to leave the doll to. Dad practically had a *shrine* erected to Doctor Tucker. I think he has every newspaper clipping, every magazine article, *anything* about him in existence. The past ten or more years of my life I've been *steeped* in the life and career of your brother. I feel I know him almost better than I know myself. What a marvelous person he is!

TRACY. Well, maybe career-wise. In person, he's more of an anxiety case.

LANGDON. Not to mention *dangerous.*

TRACY. Now-now, Langdon, Cliff wouldn't actually *carry out* any threats he might have made. He's just being big-brotherly about me.

ANNABEL. (*stands*) Do you know—all at once, I'm very nervous. It feels almost like stage-fright. Maybe I should have just *mailed* the doll, with an explanatory letter.

TRACY. (*stands, takes ANNABEL's hand*) You'll do just fine, trust me.

ANNABEL. But I feel like such an *intruder.* If I weren't so awed by your brother's reputation, I wouldn't have come at all. But I just *had* to meet this paragon of all the nicer virtues.

TRACY. *Cliff?*

ANNABEL. Dad always thought *so* highly of him. Your brother's become a kind of epitome of all that's wonderful in this world—a knight in shining armor—a holy grail—

LANGDON. Holy *terror* is more like it! The way he *looked* at me—!

TRACY. Langdon, that was brotherly love!

LANGDON. Then I'd dread to see brotherly *hate!*

ANNABEL. If only—if only *Dad* could have been here

to meet him, too . . . ! (*abruptly starts to cry, knuckling vainly under her eyes*) Excuse me. Have you got a Kleenex?

TRACY. (*takes ANNABEL's brandy glass, points* U.R.) Through that archway, past the unmade bed, and into my bathroom. Maybe you'd like to freshen up after your long trudge through the snowdrifts, anyhow.

ANNABEL. Yes. Yes, thanks, I would! (*heads that way*)

LANGDON. (sotto voce *to TRACY:*) I'm no psychologist, but it almost sounds as if Annabel's in *love* with your brother!

TRACY. (*similarly*) Well, that wouldn't be the *worst* thing that could happen to him!

ANNABEL. (*stops short of exit as JAKE emerges; asks hopefully:*) Doctor Tucker—?

JAKE. Sorry, no. But from that *look* in your eyes, I sure *wish* I was! I'm just his amiable attorney, Jake Putnam.

TRACY. (*now cradling blanket-wrapped doll on one arm*) Jake, save the chitchat for later, she has to go to the bathroom!

JAKE. (*steps aside*) Oh, sorry. (*points* U.R.) It's right through there.

ANNABEL. Thank you. (*to others:*) Be right back. (*Exits* U.R.*; JAKE starts across room toward TRACY, sees bundle, reacts*)

JAKE. Aha! So little Annabel's arrived at last! Which means—(*thumb-jerks toward* U.R.)—*that* must have been the social worker, right? What an absolute *dish*! (*will proceed to TRACY during:*) I thought all social workers wore thick glasses, no makeup, and their hair in a bun!

TRACY. Spoken like a true chauvinist! You ought to be ashamed! (*CLIFF appears on stairs, descending to foyer, during:*)

JAKE. (*reaches and gently takes doll from TRACY on:*) May *I* hold her? (*rocks it in his arms, peering at face*) What a doll! What an absolute *doll*!

LANGDON. You can say *that* again!

CLIFF. (*en route toward group, belatedly reacts to tableau*) Hey, is that *her*? My little foundling? Wow! (*hastens down and takes doll from JAKE during:*) She's so *tiny*! How in the world did she *get* here?

JAKE. With the social worker, of course!

CLIFF. (*rocking doll in his arms, peering adoringly at its face*) Oh, hell, I hope you didn't let her *leave*? I'd like to *tip* her or something — (*to JAKE:*) Or is that legal?

JAKE. Clifford my boy, social workers may find fault with *many* things in today's society, but being handed *money* isn't one of them!

CLIFF. Well, did *somebody* tip her, I hope?

TRACY. Cliff, there's something I have to tell you about this little Annabel in your arms —

CLIFF. She's so tiny — so helpless — so cute — and now, holding her, it's the strangest sort of feeling, but — I think — I think I feel — almost *fatherly*!

TRACY. (*sincerely*) Why, Cliff, I'm impressed! But I'm afraid I should tell you that —

(*door buzzer sounds; immediately, CLIFF reacts*)

CLIFF. Oh, damn, if that's *Bobbi*, I'm a dead man! (*is stepping left, right, back, etc., cradling doll*) No tux, no unfrosted bouquet, no fresh shrimp on the *hors d'oeuvre* — !

TRACY. I thought you *phoned* all those places?!

CLIFF. I've been upstairs *trying* to phone, but there's something wrong with the line! I keep getting a strange *man's* voice telling me I have a *roommate*!

TRACY. (*whirls to face LANGDON*) The *answering-*machine! Langdon, what did you *do* to it?!

LANGDON. (*heading for phone*) Search me! Maybe it's more complicated than I figured!

CLIFF. Can you *fix* it? (*door buzzer sounds again, a little longer*)

TRACY. Not in time to keep Bobbi from chewing your *head* off! (*LANGDON stops*)

CLIFF. (*inspired*) *Sick!* That's it! I was taken horribly *ill* right after she left! With the five-hour *flu* or something! Here —! (*hands doll to TRACY*) You take Annabel into your bedroom! Jake, give me a second to run upstairs and get into my bathrobe, then you get the door!

TRACY. (*moving obediently toward* U.R.) But Cliff, I still haven't explained about —

CLIFF. (*to LANGDON:*) What the hell are *you* still doing here?!

LANGDON. Having a brandy.

CLIFF. *My* brandy?!

TRACY. It was *my* idea, to calm the poor guy down. He was so afraid he'd gotten me in *trouble* that —

CLIFF. *What?!* (*door buzzer sounds again*, much *longer this time*)

TRACY. Langdon, you'd better come with *me* before he gets violent! (*Exits* U.R.)

CLIFF. (*as LANGDON almost* gallops U.R. *after her:*) You stay *out* of my sister's *bedroom!* (*gives up, rushes for stairs*) Oh, hell, I'll have to kill him *later!* I've got to get into that robe! (*thunders up stairs and out of view, just as ANNABEL comes curiously into room via* U.R., *almost collides with LANGDON exiting* U.R., *manages to keep her balance, then asks JAKE, who's headed for front door:*)

ANNABEL. What's all the excitement? I heard shouting, and —

(*buzzer sounds, and will continue to sound till door is opened*)

JAKE. No time to explain now! I'd better get that before the *windows* shatter! (*flings open door, and BOBBI storms in*)

BOBBI. *Wherrrrre* is he?!

JAKE. Now-now, Bobbi—

BOBBI. (*reacts to ANNABEL*) And who is *this*?!

JAKE. Why this is—uh—(*to ANNABEL:*) I never *did* catch your *name*—?

ANNABEL. I'm Annabel Fesco.

JAKE. (*recoils*) *Annabel Fesco*?!

BOBBI. Jake Putnam, what is the *matter* with you? And where is *Clifford*?! (*from* U.R., *we suddenly hear baby crying; BOBBI reacts*) And what in the world is *that*?

TRACY. (*pops out via* U.R. *arch, doll in her arms, calls to ANNABEL*) Sorry! It started crying and I can't make it stop!

ANNABEL. (*hurries in that direction*) Oh, here, let me show you how it's done!

BOBBI. (*as TRACY hastily re-pops back through archway, with ANNABEL following*) Jake, what is going *on* here?!

JAKE. (*still staring confusedly after the vanished AN-NABEL, as crying stops*) I'm not exactly sure *myself*—! (*then BOTH look up as CLIFF, now with his robe on, hair tousled, starts down the stairs toward them*)

BOBBI. So *there* you are, you louse! I *don't* think that telephone-gag was very *funny*!

CLIFF. (*at sea*) What are you talking about?

BOBBI. That message telling me I was wasting my time

because you already *have* a roommate! What did it mean?! What roommate? (*with sudden horrible intuition*) It's not—it's not that—that *Annabel Fesco*—?! (*flails finger toward* U.R.; *CLIFF glances that way, thinks he understands, turns back to her with a delighted smile*)

CLIFF. You *know* about her! Oh, is *that* a load off my mind! I didn't know how to begin to tell you! (*clutches her by upper arms*) Oh, Bobbi, I've got to come clean with you! I was planning to lie to you, but now that you know about Annabel, it's not important anymore!

JAKE. (*scenting disaster*) Uh—*Cliff*—

BOBBI. (*pulls free of his grasp*) *Lie* to me? Clifford, what is going *on* here?! Mother had to take a *taxi* to my apartment, and when I tried to phone you for an explanation, that stupid machine told me *not* to! And why aren't you *dressed* yet?

CLIFF. Well, you see—

BOBBI. Did you at least get your *tux*?

CLIFF. Well, uh, *no*, but—

BOBBI. (*increasingly aghast*) Did you get to the caterer's about the shrimp?

CLIFF. Uh, not quite—

BOBBI. Well, I *hope* you managed to have the man freeze or unfreeze my bridal bouquet?!

CLIFF. Not just yet, but—

BOBBI. Then just what *have* you been doing since I left here?!

CLIFF. Well, see, my car wouldn't start, so—

BOBBI. Why didn't you take a *cab*?

JAKE. You can't *get* a cab in Manhattan during a blizzard!

BOBBI. Don't be ridiculous. I *never* have any trouble getting one!

CLIFF. That's because you stand on the curbside and wave a hundred-dollar bill! Every cab within *two blocks* tries to pull up!

BOBBI. I shouldn't even *be* here! I still have that fitting to finish, and heaven-knows-*how*-many other things to attend to, but when that stupid *machine* answered—

CLIFF. (*grabs her again*) Forget the machine! Forget the tux, the shrimp, the bouquet, everything! Bobbi, I have something to tell you, something wonderful, something marvelous, something that's made me so crazily happy that—

JAKE. (*sensing what's coming*) Uh—Cliff—

BOBBI. (*made fearful by his words*) Oh, Cliff—I'm almost afraid to ask—does this have something to do with that—that *Annabel* . . . ?

CLIFF. It has *everything* to do with her! Oh, Bobbi, I had no idea how empty my life was until just a little while ago, when I picked her up—

BOBBI. Picked her up?!

JAKE. Uh—Cliff—

CLIFF. And when I held her in my arms, and looked down at that sweet little face—it was love at first sight!

BOBBI. *Love?!*

JAKE. (*a little more desperately*) Cliff!

CLIFF. Jake, will you please stop butting in, this is important!

JAKE. (*looks heavenward, shrugs*) Well—I *tried!*

BOBBI. Clifford, you can't be serious?!

CLIFF. Oh, but Bobbi, if you could have *seen* her, felt that soft and helpless body wrapped in that tiny blanket—

BOBBI. *Blanket?!*

JAKE. (*beginning to enjoy the situation very much, elaborates helpfully:*) *Tiny* blanket!

BOBBI. (*pulls from his grasp, takes backstep toward still-open door*) Clifford Tucker, what are you *telling* me?!

(*From* U.R., *obviously long since eavesdropping, a cautious ANNABEL, followed by TRACY—still holding doll—and LANGDON, all Enter, trying to figure out how to assist this foundering ship called Cliff; ANNABEL looks quite concerned, TRACY is growing as giddily amused as JAKE, and LANGDON just looks politely fascinated, as they move slowly toward foyer, during:*)

CLIFF. Look, Bobbi, I know this is a bit *sudden*, but you've always been such a good sport—

BOBBI. *Sport*?!

JAKE. *Good* sport!

BOBBI. (*flails a finger toward as-yet-unseen-by-CLIFF advancing ANNABEL*) You expect me to be a good sport about you sharing your apartment with *her*?!

CLIFF. (*turns head, reacts with blinking confusion at the sight of ANNABEL, turns back to BOBBI for:*) Why would I want *her* living with me?! (*belatedly reacts, turns, gives ANNABEL an appreciative up-and-down look, then turns back to BOBBI for:*) Let me re-phrase that. (*"baby" starts crying*) Damn, we're making too much noise! Now we woke up the baby!

BOBBI. Whose baby *is* that?!

CLIFF. (*now totally confused*) I thought you *knew*. It's mine!

BOBBI. (*again flails finger at ANNABEL, but speaks to CLIFF*) Yours and *hers*?!

ANNABEL. (*trying to help*) I just delivered it!

BOBBI. (*to ANNABEL, incredulously:*) Shouldn't you be lying *down*?

CLIFF. (*beginning to sense, though not quite understand why, doom is afoot*) Bobbi, just listen to me for a moment, there's a very simple explanation to all this! (*she waits, others wait, CLIFF just stares at her for about two seconds, then turns helplessly toward others with a bewildered shrug, on:*) . . . What *is* it?

BOBBI. You monster! You're—you're—you're not *fit* to live among penguins!

CLIFF. (*shocked, since, silly as it sounds, this is her top anathema*) Darling, you don't *mean* that!

BOBBI. Don't you *dare* call me "darling"! Clifford Tucker, right this moment—*me* or Annabel—*choose!*

CLIFF. (*heartbrokenly*) Choose?! But—I was kind of hoping to have *both* of you! (*BOBBI screams, takes a backstep, screams again, takes another backstep, her eyes locked in shocked horror on CLIFF's face; now she's in the doorway, and now she gives final long-drawn-out scream as she rushes out of our view; a stunned CLIFF just stands there, then steps to door, looks confusedly down hallway after her, then turns to face others*) Was it something I *said* . . . ?

TRACY. (*gently places a hand upon ANNABEL's shoulder*) Cliff, honey . . . *this* is Annabel Fesco!

CLIFF. (*it hasn't hit him; he looks ANNABEL up and down; then:*) But—you're a full-grown *woman!*

JAKE. And don't think *Bobbi* didn't notice.

CLIFF. (*still at sea*) Bobbi? (*semi-chuckles*) You don't mean she thought I was talking about—(*then it hits him*) Oh *noooooo!* (*and still trailing this final syllable, he turns and bolts through open doorway into hall and out of our view, in hopelessly belated pursuit of BOBBI, while JAKE starts laughing hilariously till he just plain doubles *up in happy convulsions, and TRACY—trying hard to hide her own amusement—shakes her head in a shame-shame way at JAKE, and LANGDON shrugs in his happy non-involvement status, while ANNABEL just looks from one to the other as if they're all crazy, and then:)*

ANNABEL. How *can* you just stand here and *chuckle* about this?! That poor man's *life* is being shattered, and you all treat it as some kind of *joke!*

TRACY. You're right, we *are* being callous. It's just—well, I didn't know my brother had such fatherly affection *in* him, and seeing that wonderful display of love, for a mechanical *toy,* with his life going down the drain—! *Yes,* Jake, this is a *toy* he's shattering his life for!

JAKE. *(trying to somber up a bit, prods doll she holds, reacts, then shrugs)* Don't think of it as a shattered life. Think of it as a rescue from *frostbite!* Why should my best buddy spend his honeymoon fighting *freezer*-burn?

ANNABEL. His financee wasn't *that* icy!

LANGDON. Mister Putnam means they were going to honeymoon at the South Pole!

TRACY. He may be blue *now,* but nowhere *near* as blue as he would have been *tomorrow!* *(TRACY and JAKE laugh again)*

ANNABEL. He's *got* to be told, told at *once,* that little Annabel isn't a *real* baby! Then he can *call* his fiancee and *explain—*

TRACY. She's right. Langdon, will you *please* ungimmick the answering-machine? Soon as Annabel tells him what's what, he's gonna want to phone Bobbi.

LANGDON. Will do. *(heads toward machine, which he will fiddle with, during:)*

ANNABEL. Why should *I* be the one to tell him the truth?

JAKE. 'Cause *you're* the only one who *wants* to! (*at this point CLIFF storms into foyer from hall, slams door*)

CLIFF. The elevator doors closed before I could get to her, damn it! (*will tear off robe, toss it aside, start putting on his overcoat*) I've got to—

TRACY. Cliff, relax! Langdon's fixing the phone, and you can just *call* her and explain—

CLIFF. (*abruptly pauses, then re-hangs overcoat on rack, during:*) No. No, I'm not *going* to explain. If Bobbi can be so heartless about a tiny helpless little baby, then our marriage would be a mistake! (*will come from foyer and move toward ANNABEL, during:*)

TRACY. But Bobbi didn't know you were *talking* about a baby!

JAKE. Tracy, whose side are you *on*?

CLIFF. It doesn't *matter* what she thought! The way she jumped to conclusions about me and this young lady here—what kind of trust is *that* to build a marriage on?!

ANNABEL. But she *didn't* jump, Doctor Tucker, she was being *pushed*! Those things you said—

CLIFF. (*takes her gently by the upper arms*) Not another word. I've had time to think, now, and—I want you to know—I understand.

ANNABEL. Understand *what*?

CLIFF. Jake said your father was leaving me his only *child*, not his *grandchild*. That means *you*, doesn't it! And there's only one reason a man would leave a *grownup* daughter to somebody—that daughter obviously needs help, badly. And once I saw that amazing resemblance to you in that baby's face—I figured it all out.

ANNABEL. (*catching his drift, but not annoyed enough to pull free of him*) Oh, now *wait* a minute, I know what you're thinking, and I should tell you that—

CLIFF. (*pulls her closer, in a fatherly manner*) You

don't have to conceal your secret anymore. You're among friends. I *know* you don't have a husband!

TRACY. (*fascinated*) *How* do you know?

CLIFF. Easy. Why else would her little baby's last name be "*Fesco*"?

ANNABEL. Oh, now, just a *minute*—

JAKE. (*mock-serious*) There's no point in denying the truth. Trust us, Annabel. We understand. (*tries a friendly hand on her shoulder, which gesture she avoids by pulling away from him, which puts her right into CLIFF's full embrace*)

ANNABEL. Now, *look*—

CLIFF. (*arms fully around her now*) It's all right, Annabel. I'll try not to betray your father's trust.

ANNABEL. (*so comfortable in his arms it makes her uncomfortable*) You've *got* to let me explain! See, Dad thought you were probably the nicest man in the world when it came to little children, so he wanted you to have—

CLIFF. *Forget* the past! It doesn't matter. We'll never speak of it again. From now on, your home is *here,* with *me*!

ANNABEL. (*enjoying his embrace* very *much*) You mean—forever and ever—you and me—?

CLIFF. For as long as you like. What do you say?

ANNABEL. (*trying hard to be strictly honest*) Well, listen, over the years *I've* come to admire you just as much as *Dad* did, but I *do* think there's something you absolutely *must* know, Doctor Tucker—

CLIFF. "Cliff."

ANNABEL. C-Cliff. I think you should know that little Annabel is—

LANGDON. (*turns to face group as he hangs up phone receiver*) Telephone's fixed! (*phone rings*) See?

TRACY. (*hurrying toward it, handing doll to LANG-*

DON en route) *I'll* get it, they're busy! (*grabs up receiver*) Hello?

CLIFF. Annabel, forgive the interruption. Now tell me what you were about to say. "Little Annabel is—"?

TRACY. (*cradles receiver to chest, calls across room*) Cliff, it's another Village Voice reader who wants to share the rent with you!

CLIFF. (*holds ANNABEL closer, totally fatherly and protective*) Tell the caller Doctor Tucker already *has* a roommate—for *life!* (*but TRACY doesn't, because she —and LANGDON and JAKE—all pay very close attention after CLIFF continues:*) Now, come on, Annabel, don't make me coax you. What were you just trying to tell me? Little Annabel is—*what?*

ANNABEL. (*finally succumbing to his embrace, pillows her cheek against his chest*) Little Annabel is going to *love* her new home!

(*and as TRACY shuts her eyes and shakes her head, LANGDON shrugs and—unseen by CLIFF, of course—tosses the doll toward JAKE, who catches it and gives it a triumphant kiss on the forehead, grinning gleefully, and ANNABEL just cuddles comfortably in CLIFF's arms, and CLIFF smiles his warm and tender and fatherly smile out front—*)

THE CURTAIN FALLS

End of Act One

ACT TWO

Curtain rises on CLIFF's apartment at just after six that evening. The snowfall has stopped, but some snow lingers on the lower window-corners; the sky beyond the visible buildings through the window is black, but a few of the windows are lighted. Apartment lighting itself is cheery, but of a more "artificial" look, kind of warm and golden (if your set has lamps, they should be lighted). CLIFF's overcoat is not on the rack. All empty glasses have been cleared except for a half-filled glass of milk on the table by a plate with a few remaining bits of lettuce and crumbs, at the U.S. side of the table. LANGDON's suitcase with the newspaper on top of it still stands against the wall U.S. of the fireplace.

At curtain-rise, we find ANNABEL seated before the empty plate, just wiping her lips on a napkin. TRACY is speaking on the telephone. [NOTE: If you had TRACY play the first act — as you may if you wish — in housecoat and slippers, she should be dressed now. ANNABEL is dressed as before.]

TRACY. (*on phone*) . . . Yes. Yes, thank you, that should take care of it. I appreciate it. (*hangs up, will start toward table on:*) Well, that cancels the Village Voice ad. How was the cheeseburger?

ANNABEL. Fantastic! (*calls kitchenward*) Langdon, you're a gustatorial genius!

LANGDON. (*Enters via K.D., an apron around his waist, will take her empty plate and attempt to take her milk, but she'll hold up a hand to stop this latter movement and hastily drain the rest of the glass then hand it to him, all this during the next few lines*) The dill pickle makes all the difference. Hamburger meat is pretty taste-less unless there's thin-sliced pickle on the bun.

TRACY. I can *never* get homemade cheeseburgers to taste like they do at a lunch counter. (*as he now Exits* K.D. *with glass and plate:*) You'll have to give me lessons!

LANGDON. Any time! (*is off*)

TRACY. Isn't Jake back *yet*?

ANNABEL. Nope. Maybe the Motor Club man is hav-ing problems starting the car for him. (*will give final dab to her lips with napkin, stand, and look around vaguely for a place to dispose of it*)

TRACY. Here, I'll take care of that. (*as she takes nap-kin from her, LANGDON re-enters* K.D., *now minus apron, so she hands the napkin to him*) No, you take care of it.

LANGDON. (*re-exits* K.D. *with napkin on:*) Okay, but *you* take care of the dishes! You got *ketchup* on most of *yours*!

TRACY. It's a deal, but only if *you* wash that *frying-pan*! (*then follows ANNABEL, who is moving toward sofa*) I can't *imagine* what's keeping Cliff so long. I hope he's not out front all this time trying to hail a cab!

ANNABEL. Where *was* he going, on a day like this?

TRACY. Wouldn't say. Just said he had some things to take care of and went out. It *can't* be the stuff about the tux and the caterer and all—not from the tone of *Bobbi's* voice when she screamed out of here. (*they will sit side by side on sofa, now*)

ANNABEL. You don't suppose he's—um—going over to *her* place to try and patch things up?

TRACY. How *could* he? I mean, he's offered you a home here for *life—that's* no way to win back his bride! (*LANGDON will emerge* K.D. *and start toward sofa*)

ANNABEL. I'm feeling guiltier with every passing hour.

Cliff's *got* to be told about little Annabel—but things have already gone so far that—how *can* I tell him? (*hugs herself and shivers*)

TRACY. (*just as LANGDON reaches sofa and half-sits beside the two of them*) Would you like a fire?

LANGDON. (*stops his descent, stands tall again*) I suppose you'd like *me* to start it up?

TRACY. (*leans back comfortably*) Well—you *are* a man . . .

LANGDON. (*amiably*) Chauvinist! (*will busy himself doing fire-starting things at fireplace*)

ANNABEL. Tracy—what am I going to do?

TRACY. Oh, relax, we'll tell him when the time comes. You merely helped me prove a point. Cliff was *not* all that excited about spending the rest of his life with *Bobbi!*

LANGDON. (*busy fire-starting till otherwise indicated*) *Or* visiting the South Pole!

ANNABEL. Isn't he worried about a—well—a breach-of-promise lawsuit or something?

TRACY. She can't *possibly* sue him! I mean, *she* did all the breaching. (*pauses, looks at ANNABEL; then:*) You really *go* for him don't you!

ANNABEL. I *know* it must seem crazy. But—knowing him—or, at least, knowing all *about* him—for the major portion of my adult life—when he took me in his arms—well—

TRACY. You just did what comes naturally? And you made a *lot* of people *very* happy! The woman Jake loves is no longer engaged to another man—Cliff doesn't have to push his way through the penguins—you've been offered shelter by a man you seem to adore—and *I* can stay on here and take care of Cliff without a guilty conscience.

LANGDON. So where does that leave *me*?

TRACY. Relax, Mister Barrymore, we'll work out the finer details later.

LANGDON. Not *much* later, I hope! I have *class* this evening. I could concentrate on my career a lot harder if I didn't have to worry about coming back here and finding my suitcase sitting at curbside!

ANNABEL. (*stands*) I really should go back to my hotel and get my things — I mean, I don't have so much as a *toothbrush* with me!

TRACY. Plenty of time for that before we all head for bed. Maybe I'll wander over there with you. I don't get *out* very much.

LANGDON. (*stands, and a warm firelight glow starts in fireplace*) There! *That* should warm things up. (*heads* U.R.) Excuse me while I wash my hands!

TRACY. (*still relaxed comfortably on sofa*) Don't wake up the *baby*!

LANGDON. (*stops, gives her a look*) Very funny. (*will turn and continue his exit* U.R., *during:*)

ANNABEL. That's another thing! You know what really baffles me? Not *once* has Cliff asked how come little Annabel hasn't needed her diaper changed, why I arrived here with no carrying-case full of bottles, formula, talcum —

TRACY. Men *never* think of things like that! To a man, a baby is something cute to pick up and coo at before turning it over to its mother again.

ANNABEL. Even so, we shouldn't just leave it lying on your bed. Cliff *surely* has brains enough to know it might roll over and fall!

TRACY. So why *did* you leave it there?

ANNABEL. (*stares at her; then:*) Isn't that where *you* left it?

TRACY. (*sensing her mood, comes suddenly to her feet*)

I thought *you* did! *Didn't* you? (*when ANNABEL shakes her head in wordless uneasiness:*) Then where *is* it?

LANGDON. (*emerging from* U.R. *archway*) Hey, what did you mean about waking the baby? It's not in *there* . . .

ANNABEL/TRACY. It's *not*?!

TRACY. But it's *gotta* be—!

ANNABEL. (*as both head* U.R., *fast*) Who had it last?!

TRACY. I gave it to Langdon!

LANGDON. When?!

TRACY. When *Bobbi* was heading for the hills! *No!* Right after *Cliff* came back here!

LANGDON. You did? Oh, yeah, now I remember— but *I* tossed it to *Jake*!

ANNABEL. So where did *he* put it?

LANGDON. (*shrugs*) Who knows?

TRACY. The bar! Check behind the bar! That's where Jake hangs out mostly. (*she and ANNABEL half-lean over bar from front as LANGDON stoops behind it and looks for doll; he straightens up, shaking his head*)

LANGDON. It's sure not back *here*!

TRACY. Damn! That's *another* thing I've got to confront Jake with, now! I've never in my life met such a clever sneak—even for a lawyer!

ANNABEL. Tracy, what are you talking about? (*by now, all have moved away from bar, midway toward sofa*)

TRACY. For starters, that *phone*-call I just finished accomplished more than canceling that *ad*. They told me who *placed* the ad!

ANNABEL. Jake?!

TRACY. The same! A very weird *pattern* is starting to develop here. Tell me, Annabel—just exactly *when* did your father die? (*as ANNABEL opens her mouth to reply,*

TRACY forestalls her:) Sometime last *summer*, I'll bet, right?

ANNABEL. Why — *yes*, about the end of July, but — ?

TRACY. Where are my brains! Where were *Cliff's* brains! I mean, everybody *knows* the Law moves about as fast as a snail wading through super-glue! There had to be the funeral, then the reading of the will, then *probate* for the will — !

ANNABEL. Well, yes, of course, but I still don't see — ?

TRACY. Look, probate takes up to six months — but when Jake waltzed in here today, he acted as if he'd just gotten the news this *morning!* He *had* to have known sooner than *that!*

ANNABEL. He got in touch with me about the middle of last *August*, actually, but —

TRACY. But he told you not to come around here with little Annabel until *today*, right? The day just before his unrequited love was due to marry Cliff!

ANNABEL. Uh — not *exactly* — I mean, he didn't know about little Annabel — or, to be accurate, didn't know Cliff was inheriting a *doll* and not Dad's actual *daughter* . . .

TRACY. The principle's the same. Jake was doing everything in his power to make sure the upcoming nuptials did *not* run *smoothly!* I mean, what with Cliff suddenly becoming a kind of surrogate *father*, and the phone ringing off the hook with eager roommates, matters were almost *certain* to hit a snag — !

LANGDON. Which matters certainly *did!*

TRACY. (*with grudging admiration*) Boy, I've got to *hand* it to that stinker! Machiavelli would've given him a *medal!* (*abruptly puzzled*) But come to think of it — why wasn't our front *door* being broken down by eager roommates, too?

LANGDON. Oh, that's an easy one: The ad gave the phone number, but not the address. I guess Jake figured *two* misprints would be a lot to swallow.

ANNABEL. So how *did* you find this place?

LANGDON. One of my fellow student actors works days for the phone company. I gave him the phone number and he got me the address — I figured it'd give me an edge on the competition.

TRACY. (*links arms with him, fondly*) Which it certainly did! I guess I can't be too upset with Jake about *that*!

ANNABEL. Say, aren't we getting off the track? Your brother may return at any moment, and we still haven't located little Annabel!

TRACY. Yipe! You're right! Come on, everybody, *search*! Annabel, you take the living room, Langdon check out the kitchen, I'll go rummage upstairs!

(*LANGDON will Exit* K.R., *TRACY will rush upstairs and off, and ANNABEL will glance about uncertainly, then start lifting and looking under the sofa-cushions; as she is doing so, front door opens and CLIFF Enters, humming happily, his arms laden with things like stuffed bears, dolls, other baby-toys of the genre, etc.; he spots ANNABEL, and:*)

CLIFF. Hey there, little mother! Look what Daddy Cliff got for Baby Annabel!

ANNABEL. (*springs upright, panicky*) Cliff! When did *you* come in? (*then sees toys, and her terror turns to amusement*) Oh my! You *have* been a busy shopper, haven't you! Oh, here, let me help you with those things —! (*during next few lines, she'll disencumber him a bit, and he'll manage to get his overcoat off and hung on rack, and they'll move to bar area, where they'll get toys set up in a row along countertop*) Oh, they're so *cute!* The *expression* on this bear is priceless!

LANGDON. (*emerging* K.R., *reacting to all the purchases*) Shouldn't Doctor Tucker be saying "Ho-ho-ho!"?

CLIFF. Why are *you* still here?! Can't you get it through your head that I'm *not* moving out tomorrow, so there won't be any *room* for a roommate?!

LANGDON. You know, I *asked* Tracy about that, but she seems to think —

CLIFF. You're wrong. She *never* thinks! But this is a two-bedroom condominium, and even if we can squeeze Annabel and the baby in with my sister, you are *not* sleeping with *me!* (*phone rings; galvanized, CLIFF rushes toward it, on:*) Damn, that's going to wake up the baby! (*grabs it up before it can ring a second time*) Hello! . . . (*TRACY comes hurrying down the stairs, her face anxious*)

TRACY. *I* can't find it *anywh* —! (*she cuts off in mid-syllable on getting frantic hand-signals from ANNABEL and LANGDON that CLIFF — who doesn't see them do so — is present; sighting him, she continues downstairs mutely and will converge with the others in the area just in front of the bar. NOTE: Her interjection is* brief *as possible, so that — in effect — CLIFF's on-phone conversation isn't interrupted for more than half a second, and flows from his previously spoken "Hello!" directly into this next speech with only a fractional pause; she will complete her descent, etc., during his next speech:*)

CLIFF. (*has not noticed TRACY nor heard her incompleted line, still on phone:*) . . . Bobbi?! . . . . You're kidding! . . . (*others, foregathered at bar, will listen and react accordingly to him*) You *mean* it? . . . . But—

that's simply — simply — *marvelous*!. . . Yes! . . . Yes, darling! . . . (*TRACY and ANNABEL mouth a silent echo of "Darrrrr-ling"? to each other*) That's wonderful! . . . Right! . . . See you then! (*hangs up phone, turns with a beaming smile to trio*) You're not going to believe this — !

TRACY. Try us.

CLIFF. Bobbi's *forgiven* me! She says she's *sure* it's just been some kind of misunderstanding, and she *apologized* for not giving me time to explain!

TRACY. Apologized? Bobbi Ralston?!

CLIFF. They're going to come over here, just as planned, and she said I can explain things to her *then*!

TRACY. (*horrified*) What? Come over? *Who*? Cliff, you don't mean Bobbi and her *mother* — the third-richest woman on this *planet*?!

CLIFF. (*baffled by her attitude*) What are you so upset about? It didn't bother you when she was *originally* scheduled to come over her tonight — ?

TRACY. Clifford, you numbskull! *That* was because I planned to go *shopping*, get my *hair* done, cook up bunches of super-fancy *food*, *clean* this place — ! What the hell am I going to do *now*?!

LANGDON. (*helpfully*) Does Mrs. Ralston like cheeseburgers — ?

OTHERS. (*aghast*) *Cheeseburgers*?

LANGDON. (*abashed*) I was *only* trying to *help* . . .

TRACY. (*impulsively gives him a brief embrace, on:*) Of course you were! Come to think of it — maybe you *can* help!

CLIFF. Him? How?

TRACY. (*to LANGDON:*) Hustle right over to the nearest store, buy up *anything* that looks fancy enough for *rich* people to eat, get back here and start *fixing* it!

That'll give me time enough to at least *comb* my hair and get into a fancier dress —

LANGDON. Tracy, what'll I use for *money?*

TRACY. Cliff, give the man some money!

CLIFF. Right! (*will fumble out wallet and hand fistful of bills to him, during:*) I really appreciate this, kid, and I promise you — if everything goes well tonight — I'll fix those *ears* of yours for *free!* (*LANGDON, not sure if he's being rewarded or insulted, tentatively brings his finger-tips to his ears, but then drops them and takes money, on:*)

LANGDON. My *mother* says I have *beautiful* ears . . .

CLIFF. (*heading for sofa area*) Bring her over. I'll fix her *eyes!*

TRACY. (*headed for stairs*) Langdon, there's a super-fancy deli just at the end of the block! Get going! (*will ascend stairs and vanish, during:*)

LANGDON. I'll do my best — ! (*will head for front door, money in fist*) What kind of food do rich people *like?*

TRACY. (*off*) *Anything expensive!*

LANGDON. Right! (*Exits to hall, shutting door after him*)

ANNABEL. (*who has remained in bar area, looking numb, now moves toward sofa area*) You must be — very relieved, Cliff . . .

CLIFF. (*warming his hands at the fire, stops, turns her way*) Well, who *wouldn't* be? (*will move to meet her just below sofa, and take her hands, during:*) The ghastliest day of my life has just turned into a bucket of roses! I'll explain to Bobbi about you and little Annabel, her mother will give her approval of me and the marriage, the wedding will go off without a hitch, and then — (*abruptly does a 180-degree shift in mood, dropping her hands and dropping down onto sofa, his voice becoming an anguished sob, on:*) I don't *want* to go to the South Po-o-o-ole! I *hate* the cold! I hate *penguins!* (*a super-wail on:*) *I* don't even like *Bobbiiiiii*—! (*buries his face in his hands and weeps piteously*)

ANNABEL. (*drops down beside him, embracing him, cradling his head*) Cliff, what are you *saying?* Why did you ever get *engaged* to her if you—?

CLIFF. (*very maudlin, clutching her for support, choking out his words*) It was the clinic—the clinic I want to build so little kids without money can get free plastic surgery—but *I* can't afford to endow a place like that—and Bobbi knows all the rich people in the world—she could get donations *flying* in—and—and—(*will recover some semblance of control*) Bobbi's not bad-*looking* or anything—nice enough personality—we've known one another for years and years—marriage to her wouldn't be absolutely *ghastly* or anything—except—except—oh, Annie, what am I going to *do?!*

ANNABEL. Tell Bobbi the truth!

CLIFF. (*miserably*) That's very virtuous, but not the least bit practical.

ANNABEL. But you can't marry a woman you don't love!

CLIFF. Of course I can. It's done every day.

TRACY. (*appears on stairs, flustered, will head for her room during:*) Why did I go up*stairs? My* room is *down*stairs! (*reacts to twosome on sofa, stops just short of bar*) What's going on here?

ANNABEL. He's complaining, I'm comforting.

TRACY. (*hasn't really heeded, too intent on dressing up, heads* U.R. *again*) Good, good. See ya!

CLIFF. Be *quiet* in there, or you'll waken the baby! (*this reminds both women simultaneously; ANNABEL comes*

*to her feet, a hand to her mouth in horrified remem-
brance; TRACY stops just before bar)*

TRACY. Uh . . . *right!* Mousy quiet. I'll even dress in
the dark! (*exchanges panicky look with ANNABEL, then
as CLIFF turns to face ANNABEL again, is suddenly
inspired—looks at array of stuffed toys on bar—makes
a decision—grabs a small baby-sized stuffed monkey—
exits* U.R., *all during:*)

CLIFF. (*on re-facing ANNABEL*) What's the matter?
You look absolutely ghastly!

ANNABEL. (*hastily re-sits beside him*) It's nothing.
Nothing at all. I'm all right now.

CLIFF. But what *was* it?

ANNABEL. I'm—I'm upset about you marrying Bobbi
Ralston! I don't *want* you to marry Bobbi!

CLIFF. *You* don't? Annie, that's very sympathetic of
you, but—

ANNABEL. Sympathy has nothing to do with it!

CLIFF. Then *why* don't you want me to marry Bobbi?

ANNABEL. Because—because I want you to marry
me!

CLIFF. (*stunned*) *What*?!

ANNABEL. (*mis-reading him*) Is the prospect *that*
horrifying?

CLIFF. Horrifying? I'm not horrified—I'm shocked!
No, wait, that sounds too much like disapproval. And I
don't disapprove of the idea at all. Except that if I
dumped Bobbi *now,* she'd sue the pants off me! Besides
—I only just *met* you today!

ANNABEL. *I* only just met *you* today. *I'm* game, why
not *you*?

CLIFF. (*wonderingly*) You're *serious* about this, aren't
you! Annie, you surprise me.

ANNABEL. You're not half so surprised as *I* am.

CLIFF. But — be logical — how could you expect me to think of marrying a woman I've known for less than ten hours?

ANNABEL. It's not too much to expect — you *are* thinking about it.

CLIFF. Annie, this is crazy.

ANNABEL. Why? Let me put it this way: Do you like me better than Bobbi?

CLIFF. Yes. Yes I do. A lot better.

ANNABEL. Well, then, if you're willing to marry a woman you like *less* than me, why not *me*?

CLIFF. (*stares out front, confused*) Because it — it — it just isn't *done*!

ANNABEL. Aw, Cliff — (*cuddles near him*) I didn't say marry me *tomorrow* — just *eventually*, when you think the time is right.

CLIFF. Now, *that's* a *lot* more reasonable! Let's *date* awhile, find out a little more *about* one another, weigh the pros and cons. That's the *normal* way to do it.

ANNABEL. *Not* when the man you want is about to leave for the South Pole with his *bride*!

CLIFF. (*finally gets it*) *Oh!* So *that's* why you came on so strong so suddenly!

ANNABEL. What *else* could I do? Like the old song says, there wasn't much *time* for the waiting game! Telling you how I felt, so soon, was the hardest thing I ever had to do in my entire life! But how *could* I wait? By tomorrow, you'll be married and gone!

CLIFF. (*stares at her for a long moment; then:*) That's what *you* think! (*grabs her in his arms and kisses her, good; breaks, and:*) Now, don't you *dare* say "This is so sudden"! (*kisses her again, and she helps, and then door buzzer sounds*)

ANNABEL. (*comes to her feet, panicky*) It's Bobbi!

CLIFF. (*stands, embraces her, shakes his head*) Impossible. Even waving *thousand*-dollar bills, she couldn't get here so fast! (*starts for door*) I'll see who it is — *you* start figuring out what you're going to *wear* tonight!

ANNABEL. You mean for the meet-Mrs.-*Ralston* party?! I didn't know I was *invited*!

CLIFF. Of course you are! I need *you* to *corroborate* things when I explain to Bobbi!

ANNABEL. Cliff, are you nuts?! If you *explain* to her, you'll have to *marry* her!

CLIFF. (*just at door, pauses as this sinks in*) I never *thought* of that! Annie, what am I going to do? (*door buzzer sounds*) Oh, damn. Excuse me! (*opens door, LANGDON hurries in with two large grocery bags, heads for* K.R.)

LANGDON. Thanks, these things weigh a ton! (*as he continues cross and Exits:*)

ANNABEL. Cliff! I can't *possibly* attend that party! I have nothing to wear!

CLIFF. I thought you didn't *want* to attend?

ANNABEL. Well, I'm certainly not going to leave you alone here with *Bobbi*! (*starts for* U.R.) Maybe Tracy has something suitable I can borrow.

CLIFF. What do you mean, "suitable"? You look just fine!

ANNABEL. To meet *you*, yes — *not* to meet the third-richest woman in the world! (*dashes off via* U.R. *archway*)

LANGDON. (*comes out of kitchen, crosses toward suitcase*) That reminds me, *I'd* better get changed, myself!

CLIFF. What do *you* care how you look tonight?

LANGDON. (*business of getting suitcase and heading for stairs*) Rebecca Ralston is rich. Rich ladies are buggy about the fine arts. I'm an actor. Who knows, if I play my cards right, I could end up getting an endowment! (*is now ascending stairs*)

CLIFF. Where are you going?

LANGDON. I've got to change *someplace*!

CLIFF. In *my* bedroom?

LANGDON. Would you rather I changed in Tracy's? (*vanishes*)

CLIFF. (*belatedly*) Well, if you put it *that* way . . .

TRACY. (*rushes out via* U.R., *now dressed terrifically*) Where's Langdon? They'll be here any minute!

CLIFF. Relax, Sis! He's back, he brought the goodies, and he's upstairs changing.

TRACY. Oh, good! I think I need a drink. No, I'd better not. She'd smell it on my breath. But if I don't have one, I won't be able to talk to her. But if I do, I might start slurring my words. But if I don't, I won't know what to say, anyway—!

CLIFF. Tracy, you're *talking* to yourself!

TRACY. Then I'd *better* have a drink! Maybe *that'll* shut me up! (*but as she starts to go behind bar, ANNA-BEL runs in via* U.R.)

ANNABEL. Tracy, none of your things will *fit* me!

TRACY. Then you'll just have to go back to your *hotel* and change. It might work in your favor—if they arrive before you get back, you can make a Grand Entrance!

ANNABEL. In my *jogging*-suit? I didn't *bring* anything fancy with me. I thought I'd just drop off little Annabel and be on the next flight out of town!

CLIFF. Damn! And *I* certainly don't have anything you can wear!

(*LANGDON appears on stairs, same trousers as before, but now his light canvas jacket has been replaced by a*

*slick dinner-jacket, and his boots by nicely shined
loafers; he's heard CLIFF's line and replies to it:)*

LANGDON. Hey, maybe *I* have! Annabel, hurry upstairs and look in my suitcase, it's open on the bed.

ANNABEL. (*heading that way despite misgivings*)
Langdon, are you sure? What can you possibly have that
I could wear?

LANGDON. My best dress! (*others pause where they are
and just look at him; he stops at foot of stairs and jams his
fists against his hips in chagrin*) From a *play* I was in back
home! I don't *normally* wear a dress.

TRACY. Well, thank heaven for *that*! Go on, Annabel,
you haven't much time!

ANNABEL. Right! Thanks, Langdon! (*vanishes
upstairs*)

CLIFF. Maybe *I* should change! No, wait, I don't *want*
to impress Mrs. Ralston! But on the other hand, I don't
want to embarrass *Bobbi*! But on the other hand—

TRACY. Cliff, you've only *got* two hands! Langdon,
don't just stand there, get out in the kitchen and start
cooking!

LANGDON. Right! (*heads for* K.R.)

CLIFF. Langdon, what play *was* it? *Charley's Aunt*?

TRACY. I *hope* not! Today's fashions have progressed a
bit beyond the *bustle*!

LANGDON. Don't worry, the outfit is as modern as you
can get! (*Exits via* K.R.)

CLIFF. That's a relief! What show *was* it?

LANGDON. (*off*) *La Cage aux Folles*!

CLIFF/TRACY. *Whaaat*?! (*door buzzer sounds*)

CLIFF. (*reacts with panic*) It's Bobbi!

TRACY. It can't be! She's too early—even for *Bobbi*!

LANGDON. (*pops out* K.R.) Shall *I* get the door?

TRACY. Get back in there and *cook*! (*he pops back*) Cliff, you've *got* to answer it. Bobbi must have a *thumb-callus* after *today's* visits!

CLIFF. Or she thinks we all have *hearing*-problems! . . . Oh, what the hell! (*opens door, then sags in relief as a jubilant JAKE walks in, now dressed in an elegant suit-and-tie*) Jake! Where did you change clothes, in the parking garage?!

JAKE. (*sashaying proudly into room, moving toward bar*) As a matter of fact, yes! I always carry a spare suit in the trunk of my car, in case unexpected business crops up when I'm driving casual.

TRACY. (*has already stepped behind bar and is pouring him a drink*) Even so, it's going a bit far even for a *lawyer* to dress up for the man from the Motor Club!

JAKE. Oh, *that* was taken care of *hours* ago! I had *legal* business to attend to!

CLIFF. I thought you took today *off*, what with the bachelor party last night and the wedding tomorrow. (*will close front door and start moving toward bar after JAKE*)

JAKE. Ah, but something important came up! I got to thinking—*why* is everyone having problems today? And all at once, I realized what the problem *was*, and how to *solve* it! (*takes drink from TRACY*) Thanks. (*takes a sip, then sets glass on bar and turns to just-arriving CLIFF*) Buddy-boy, old friend, you are about to become the happiest man on this planet!

CLIFF. I *am*? Jake, what are you *talking* about?

JAKE. (*clasps CLIFF by the upper arms, then announces gleefully:*) I just sold Little Annabel!

CLIFF. (*goggle-eyed*) You did *what*?!

JAKE. Don't you *get* it, buddy? Your troubles are *over*!

CLIFF. Your *life* is over! (*lunges and gets death-throttle on JAKE's neck; TRACY gallops around from behind bar and tries to separate them, during:)*

JAKE. *(barely understandable)* Cliff . . . stop . . . what're you doing—?!

CLIFF. *(busy strangling JAKE, despite TRACY's fingers prying at his grip)* How *could* you?! You *monster!* Yes, there were *problems* because she arrived here, but to take a helpless little waif and treat her like a piece of *real estate*—! *(TRACY will ad-lib, overlapping foregoing line, things akin to "Wait! Stop! You're killing him! You don't understand!", etc.)*

JAKE. *(strangulated, wide-eyed to TRACY:)* Traceeee! Didn't you *tell* him—?!

CLIFF. *(releases JAKE, gapes at his sister)* *You* knew?! You *knew* he was out selling that helpless little baby, and you didn't *tell* me—?! *(his fingers leap forward toward her throat, but she backsteps, and:)*

TRACY. Little Annabel is *not* a baby!

CLIFF. *(this stops him)* She's *what*?

JAKE. *(rubbing throat, recovering his voice)* Not . . . a . . . *baby!* I was *sure* they would have explained things to you by *now!*

CLIFF. Explained what? What things? What's going on here, anyhow?

JAKE. You didn't inherit a daughter, you inherited a *doll!*

TRACY. James Lomax Fesco was an *inventor!*

JAKE. His daughter Annabel was just *delivering* the doll!

TRACY. But you never let anybody get a word in edgewise to *tell* you about it, and by the time we *could* get a word in, things had already gone too far!

CLIFF. I must be losing my mind! This is insane! Why would Fesco leave me a *doll*?

JAKE. The confusion's *my* fault. I mis-read his last will and testament. He wasn't leaving you his child — he was leaving you his *brain*-child!

CLIFF. But she — she looked so *real* —?!

TRACY. That's the whole *point*! She's almost *undetectable* from a real baby! A toy like that is worth *millions*!

JAKE. *Multi*-millions! That's what I meant when I came in here: Your troubles are over! With the money from the sale of little Annabel, *you* can build your *own* clinic!

CLIFF. (*staggered*) I *can*? You mean — if I can do it myself — you're telling me that — that —

JAKE. You *don't* have to marry *Bobbi* to get that financial backing!

TRACY. *Or* go to the South Pole!

CLIFF. Wait — a little slower — this is all happening too fast — !

LANGDON. (*pops in via* K.R.) Food's in the microwave! Should be done in about eight minutes!

TRACY. Where were *you* when I was fighting off the Boston Strangler?!

LANGDON. You told me to *cook*! I was cooking!

CLIFF. Jake, I still don't understand — if little Annabel belonged to *me*, how could *you* sell her?

JAKE. I'm your lawyer. You gave me your power-of-attorney *years* ago! The contract'll be drawn up next Monday, and your money troubles are over forever!

TRACY. Drawn up where?

JAKE. This buddy of mine is the head of the legal department at a toy-manufacturer's. I took little Annabel downstairs with me when I went to meet the Motor Club guy, got the car started, drove over there, and made the sale in under fifteen minutes!

CLIFF. But what are we going to tell *Bobbi*?

JAKE. Bobbi? What are you talking about? What's *she* got to do with any of this?

TRACY. She's going to *arrive* here at any moment!

LANGDON. With her rich mother.

JAKE. What the hell *for*?! I thought the engagement was finished — over — *kaput*?

CLIFF. Bobbi changed her mind.

TRACY. It's a woman's prerogative.

JAKE. But — this is *terrible*! If *you* break the engagement, I'll have to *sue* you!

LANGDON. *You* will?

CLIFF. Jake's *Bobbi's* lawyer, too!

TRACY. That's how they *met* — in Jake's waiting room.

JAKE. (*pounds his fist into his palm*) *Why* did I keep her *waiting* that day?! *Why*?!

CLIFF. Jake, why are *you* so upset about the wedding? It's *my* problem, isn't it?

TRACY. Not when your best man is in love with your bride-to-be!

CLIFF. Jake! Why didn't you *tell* me?

JAKE. 'Cause you're my best friend in all the world! If you knew I loved your bride — things would get pretty awkward.

CLIFF. (*lighting up*) Hey! That's our *answer*! If *you* can persuade Bobbi to marry *you*, *I* won't have to!

JAKE. Do you think I *can* — ?

TRACY. What've you got to *lose*?

JAKE. But how can I possibly make time with Bobbi at her engagement party to *you*?

CLIFF. Tell her you're crazy about *penguins*! She *knows* that *I'm* not!

JAKE. Will it *work*?

TRACY. (*shrugs*) It's a *start* . . .

(and then ANNABEL appears, and stops, at the head of the stairs, looking down at group; she must be wearing all the silk, satin, gauze, sequins, bugle-beads and maribou feathers in existence; from headdress to hem, she shimmers and glares and sparkles in every color of the rainbow; her face is a study in muted misery; since her appearance is a guaranteed laugh, she should hold for the laugh, and then speak as it fades:)

ANNABEL. How do I look? *(others turn, and—except for LANGDON, who seems pleased as punch—they give a unified* scream *and horrified simultaneous backstep from her; she looks at their stricken faces a second, nods, and says sincerely)* That's what I thought. *(turns and starts to Exit upstairs, but stops for:)*

CLIFF. Where are you going?

ANNABEL. I'm not sure. I may kill myself.

TRACY. Nonsense! You look just *fine!* Come on down here and stop being so silly!

ANNABEL. If I look so fine, why did you all scream?

JAKE. There was—so *much* fineness—all at *once*—without *warning*—!

CLIFF. We were sort of—overwhelmed.

ANNABEL. *(hesitantly turns, starts down a few steps, then pauses)* You're not putting me on?

LANGDON. Of *course* they're not! You look absolutely gorgeous! *(this relieves her, and she completes descent, not quite realizing what he's adding until he's added it all:)* All you need is a spotlight and tap-shoes!

ANNABEL. *(on foyer-level, belatedly reacts)* There! I knew it! I look like a walking *Christmas*-tree!

CLIFF. *(hurries to her before she can rush upstairs, takes her hand)* Annie, you look like a fairy princess!

ANNABEL. Really . . . ?

JAKE. I haven't seen anything so spectacular-looking since the arrival of the Good Witch of the North!

ANNABEL. (*reluctantly allowing CLIFF to lead her down to others*) But I feel so — *garish* . . .

TRACY. You want to outshine *Bobbi,* don't you?

ANNABEL. Yes, but with *charm* — not like a *lighthouse*!

CLIFF. Honey, you're going to render her *speechless*!

JAKE. And with Bobbi, that's not *easy*! (*a loud ding comes from the kitchen*)

LANGDON. Whoops, the food's ready! (*heads for* K.R.) Where do you keep the serving-dishes? (*will continue on and Exit* K.R. *during:*)

TRACY. The cabinet over the refrigerator!

ANNABEL. Cliff — before Bobbi and her mother arrive — there's something I've *got* to tell you about little Annabel!

CLIFF. You don't have to. Jake and Tracy just straightened me out. And there's something *I* have to tell *you* about her! Jake just sold her to a toy-manufacturer!

ANNABEL. As — as "Annabel *Fesco*"?

JAKE. That's the name your father wanted — that's the name she's gonna have!

ANNABEL. (*flings her arms about him and plants a kiss on his cheek*) Oh, Jake, that's *wonderful*! (*then abruptly turns to CLIFF*) I hope you don't mind finding out that I'm *not* an unwed mother — ?

CLIFF. (*as if somberly*) It *was* a terrible shock — (*holds out his arms*) — but I'll survive somehow! (*she springs into his embrace and they kiss*)

JAKE. Hey, what's going *on* here?

TRACY. I hope you didn't think penguins were the *only* reason he wants to dump Bobbi?

JAKE. (*looks at the smoochers in admiration*) Well, I'll be darned!

(*door buzzer sounds; CLIFF and ANNABEL spring apart*)

TRACY. They're *here*! (*starts toward foyer*) Battle stations, everybody!

LANGDON. (*pops out* K.R.) Hey, does that big silver platter have some kind of *lid* someplace?

TRACY. (*turns his way*) Same cabinet, way in the back!

LANGDON. Gotcha! (*re-pops*)

TRACY. (*turns toward door again, reaches for knob, then frowns and calls* K.R.:) What do you need the *lid* for?

LANGDON. (*off*) To hide my *surprise*!

CLIFF. *What* surprise?

JAKE. Bobbi doesn't *like* surprises!

ANNABEL. Then why am I wearing this *dress*?! (*door buzzer sounds again, a bit longer*)

TRACY. Oh, damn! (*turns toward door again, but before she can open it:*)

CLIFF. *Wait*! We need the *baby*!

ANNABEL. What for?

CLIFF. To explain things to Bobbi!

JAKE. The doll doesn't talk *that* good!

CLIFF. I mean, to *show* her, when *I* explain matters!

TRACY. Can't you just *tell* her about it?

JAKE. Yeah, why do you actually need it on hand?!

CLIFF. Because *Bobbi's* expecting a *baby*!

ANNABEL. *Don't* say that in front of her *mother*!

TRACY. Oh, for heaven's sake —! Wait here a minute

—maybe *I* can help! (*will hightail it toward* U.R. *and out, during:*)

JAKE. If Tracy comes back out here in a diaper, I'm going home.

LANGDON. (*pops out* K.R.) *I'm* not!

CLIFF. Will *you* get back to *work!*

LANGDON. Sorry! (*re-pops; almost simultaneously, TRACY comes rushing out via* U.R., *a cradled object* [*Oh, all right: It's the stuffed monkey.*] *swathed in a large white beach towel, looking very baby-like, indeed*)

TRACY. This will have to do! (*door buzzer starts continuously, will continue till door is opened*) Take this, Cliff, and I hope you're satisfied! (*slams it into his arms, then races to front door*)

CLIFF. (*lifts face-flap, reacts*) Tracy, this looks like a stuffed *monkey!*

TRACY. (*shrugs*) So little Annabel had a hard day!

(*yanks open door* [*buzzer stops*] *before he can respond, and then all are on their best "party behavior" as an angry BOBBI Enters, followed by REBECCA RALSTON, a short, pudgy and cute lady in her 60s, holding a lorgnon* [*sort of a fancy pince-nez*] *to her eyes, peering myopically at the assemblage* [*NOTE: the lorgnon should be on a short gold chain ending in a fancy brooch on her bosom, so she doesn't have to hold it in her hand all the time; she needs it only when trying hard to see something; to save lengthy stage-directions, every time REBECCA "peers" she is using her lorgnon*]; *both are very dressy and look fully as rich as they are*)

BOBBI. What *is* it about that *buzzer* of yours?! How many rings does it *take* to get in?

TRACY. (*instantly*) Three. We *never* open the door unless the caller rings three times. It's a sort of *code* we have with our friends, to save us from vacuum-cleaner salesmen.

BOBBI. (*since this makes sense, is instantly mollified*) Oh! Clifford, why didn't you *tell* me?

CLIFF. (*may as well go along with things*) I thought you *knew*? I mean, you always *do* ring three times when you come over.

REBECCA. Aren't you going to introduce me? (*RE-BECCA has two voices: one is "sweet," one has an "edge"; this is "edge"*)

BOBBI. Oh, I'm so sorry, this is my mother!

TRACY. *That's* nothing to be sorry about. (*before BOBBI can formulate a reply:*) How do you *do*, Mrs. Ralston. I'm Tracy Tucker, Cliff's sister. (*will indicate each person in turn:*) And this is Cliff's lawyer Jake Putnam, and this is Cliff himself, and—

REBECCA. (*peers at ANNABEL, still at an unfocused distance*) Why haven't you taken your *tree* down?

ANNABEL. (*winces, but says graciously:*) My name is Annabel Fesco.

REBECCA. (*turns to TRACY*) You have a talking tree?

TRACY. Doesn't everybody? (*will move behind REBECCA and shut front door, even as BOBBI takes her mother by the arm and leads her toward ANNABEL, on:*)

BOBBI. Tracy is just attempting to be amusing, Mother. This is a real human being, Annabel Fesco. She's only *dressed* like a Christmas tree!

ANNABEL. (*graciously taking REBECCA's hand*) You should see me on *Flag Day*!

REBECCA. (*laughs [her laugh is a kind of sharp-but-amused snort]*) Say, I *like* this girl!

BOBBI. But Mother—this is the one I was *telling* you about!

REBECCA. I *still* like her!

ANNABEL. *Thank* you, Mrs. Ralston.

REBECCA. Make it "Rebecca" — I always *did* admire a flashy dresser! (*turns to CLIFF*) So *you're* the idiot who's let Bobbi talk him into honeymooning at the South Pole! You must really be *nuts* about her — or maybe just nuts. (*peers at bundle*) What's *that* you're carrying?

BOBBI. It's that *baby* I told you about! *Now* do you see why I wanted to break off our engagement?!

TRACY. (*has rejoined group by now — they're mostly clustered right of sofa*) You mean this reconciliation is your *mother's* idea?

BOBBI. Mother doesn't *have* ideas — Mother has *ultimatums*!

REBECCA. Don't be a fool, Bobbi! You're not getting any younger, you know. Besides, he reminds me of your late father. Now *there* was one fine-looking man!

(*a curious LANGDON, unnoticed by group, will emerge* K.R. *and make his way across room to the outer fringe of group, during:*)

CLIFF. Why, *thank* you, Mrs. Ralston. You're very kind.

REBECCA. Well, if *you're* very kind, will you please offer me a *chair*? I've spent half the day flying here on the Concorde, and my jet-lag is *killing* me! (*even as others fumble ad-libs of the oh-of-course and please-sit-down variety, she ensconces herself comfortably on* R. *end of sofa; then:*) Here, let *me* hold the little tyke! (*CLIFF — with some unease — will hand bundle to her, during:*) Haven't had a baby in my arms since *Bobbi* was born — and that's an *awfully* long time ago!

BOBBI. *Really,* Mother! (*starts for bar*) I'm going to have a drink!

JAKE. (*galvanized, rushes to precede her and will get behind bar when they arrive*) Here, let *me* fix it for you, Bobbi!

REBECCA. (*lifts flap, peers at face within, then looks from ANNABEL to CLIFF, on:*) Doesn't much resemble *either* of you. Consider yourselves lucky!

ANNABEL. Oh, we *do,* we *do!*

LANGDON. Where did the baby *come* from?

TRACY. (*grabs his arm, starts steering him toward* K.R.) A fine obstetrician *you'd* make!

LANGDON. (*sotto voce*) But the three of searched this place from top to bottom for her—?!

TRACY. (*not quite as undetectably soft*) I'll *explain* to you in the *kitchen!*

REBECCA. (*peers*) Explain *what?* Who *is* this guy you're hustling out of the room?

TRACY. (*trapped, stops, and babbles:*) It's my . . . I mean, it's our . . . I mean, it's—(*inspired*) The *caterer!* We thought you'd like something really *fancy* to eat! (*to LANGDON, as a heavy-handed hint:*) Isn't that right . . . "*Pierre*"?!

LANGDON. (*catches the ball*) Oh . . . oh, *oui, madame!*

REBECCA. You mean "*ma'm'selle*"!

LANGDON. (*very uneasy*) You speak *French?*

REBECCA. I live all year round in a *chateau* in the south of France—I damn well *better* speak it, or they'd rob me blind!

LANGDON. (*trying to back toward* K.R., *doing an awkward job of it*) Ain't it *la verité!* Well, uh—*bon jour!*

REBECCA. "Good morning"?

LANGDON. I mean, *bonne nuit!*

REBECCA. "Good night"?

LANGDON. (*almost at* K.R. *now*) I mean — *bon appetit!* (*bolts from view*)

TRACY. (*fluttering gaily*) Aren't Frenchmen cute!

REBECCA. If he's French, I'm a horse's patoot! Did you check his credentials?

TRACY. I didn't *have* to! That is, I mean, he *cooks* like a *dream!* What *else* do I have to know about him?

REBECCA. Apparently, you've never heard the story of *Typhoid Mary!*

BOBBI. (*who has been seated at bar, nursing drink JAKE gave her, and chatting [unheard] with him till now*) I *hope* you're not going to *tell* it?!

ANNABEL. (*who has by now sat down at REBECCA's left on sofa, though CLIFF still kind of hovers anxiously, standing to REBECCA's right, watching the bundle*) *I've* never heard it. Who *is* she, Rebecca?

REBECCA. Well, there was this cook, named Mary, early in this century, who was naturally immune to typhus, but she changed jobs a lot, and every household where she'd worked, the people *all* came down with typhoid fever, and — (*at this point, REBECCA lets the bottom end of the beach towel slip open, and the monkey's tail — tucked up from view by TRACY — now uncurls into her lap; she peers at it uncertainly, then turns her head to CLIFF*) It's a damn good thing you're a plastic surgeon!

CLIFF. (*grabs bundle from her, hastily retucking tail from view*) Yes, isn't it!

REBECCA. (*raises her voice a bit, since he's backing away*) Listen, while you're at it, do something about that poor creature's *ears!*

LANGDON. (*pops out* K.R., *miffed*) I *heard* that!

TRACY. (*whirls to face him, blurts:*) Not *your* ears, Dumbo! The *monkey's!*

BOBBI. (*jumps off bar stool*) That's a *monkey*?! But this morning, it cried like a baby!

JAKE. (*hastening around bar to her*) You'd cry like a baby, *too*, if someone was going to amputate *your* tail!

ANNABEL. She probably *did*!

BOBBI. Now, *listen*, sister—!

REBECCA. (*edge*) *Stop*! (*has risen to her feet on the line; others all look her way*) I will have *no* petty bickering at this party. Everyone put the gloves away, and relax. Bobbi and Cliff are engaged, and they will be married tomorrow, and that's that, and I don't want to hear talk of anything else! (*sweet*) Now, what have we got to *eat*?

LANGDON. (*stands tall, proudly ticks items off in his fingers:*) We have *paté de foie gras*, we have truffles, we have *marrons glacées*, we have *petits fours* —*éclairs*—*napoléons*—*quiche*—!

CLIFF. (*staggered*) And a *very* happy proprietor at the corner *deli*!

REBECCA. But all that stuff is *French*!

TRACY. You *live* in the south of France—don't you *like* French cuisine?

REBECCA. Not three-hundred-sixty-five days a *year*! Give me a break! What I'd *really* like to sink my dentures into is a huge, juicy, high-cholesterol, genuine all-American *cheeseburger*!

LANGDON. (*with a scowl at TRACY*) *Now* she tells me!

TRACY. (*trying to save the moment*) Well, listen, Mrs. Ralston, if it's *cheeseburgers* you want, there's no better cheeseburger on this *planet* than the ones *Langdon* makes!

BOBBI. Who is *Langdon*?

LANGDON. *I* am!

REBECCA. (*to TRACY:*) I thought you said "Pierre"?

TRACY. I thought a French caterer would *impress* you! Boy, was *I* wrong!

REBECCA. (*to LANGDON:*) Young man, just exactly what *is* your name?

LANGDON. Lionel Barrymore.

REBECCA. (*peers*) You look much *older* in the *movies!*

TRACY. We're wasting time! Langdon, go make the lady a cheeseburger!

LANGDON. I can't. We're all out of ground beef.

TRACY. There was *ten pounds* of it in the freezer this morning!

BOBBI. *Ten pounds?!*

TRACY. (*with an apologetic smile*) I got a bargain last week on six boxes of Hamburger Helper.

ANNABEL. Langdon, we couldn't have eaten *all* that, today!

LANGDON. We didn't. I used what was left for my *pièce de résistance!*

JAKE. I *hope* he didn't put it in the eclairs!

REBECCA. Will you all quit this merry chit-chatting? I'm *starving!*

CLIFF. (*with sudden fury*) *Who cares?!* (*others all gasp and recoil from him, with the exception of REBECCA*)

REBECCA. (*laughs*) You know, Clifford, you even *sound* like my late husband! He'd *never* take the kind of guff I dish out!

BOBBI. Mother—you mean you're not *mad?*

REBECCA. On the contrary. I'm happier than *ever* that you're marrying this man tomorrow. *He'll* keep you in your place, all right!

TRACY. If he can ever get a *word* in!

BOBBI. Now, *just* a minute—!

REBECCA. Oh, relax, Bobbi, you *do* babble on like a senatorial filibuster! Her late *father* once described her as "one-hundred-thirty pounds of *jaw* set at *automatic*"!

BOBBI. (*stung, stands silent a second, then says in limp defense:*) One-hundred-*twenty* pounds.

JAKE. One-hundred-twenty *gorgeous* pounds!

BOBBI. Why — *thank* you, Jake . . . ? (*looks at him as if for the first time*) I didn't imagine you even *noticed* me, all these years.

JAKE. (*takes her hands*) From your first affadavit to your last pre-nuptial agreement!

BOBBI. (*abruptly pulls her hands away*) The *wedding!* I nearly forgot!

CLIFF. *I* didn't! (*thrusts monkey into TRACY's hands [during his spiel, she'll hand it impatiently to JAKE, who'll pass it similarly to BOBBI, who'll toss it onto the bar in meticulous disgust], and confronts REBECCA*) Listen, Mrs. Ralston — with all due respect — surely it's become obvious to you that, whatever I'd once planned to do, I no longer have any interest in marrying your daughter Bobbi — and, for reasons I still cannot fathom, it's become obvious that *Bobbi* has no interest in marrying *me*. Under those circumstances, I simply can't imagine why *you* continue to insist that we *do* get married.

REBECCA. (*edge*) Because *nobody* jilts a *Ralston!* The announcements have been made, the church has been booked, the invitations sent out, and the pre-nuptial agreements signed. Our family would look *foolish* were we to call the whole thing off now. I won't *have* that!

BOBBI. But Mother, *I* don't care if we look foolish. I'd *rather* look foolish than marry a man I don't dearly love!

TRACY. Then why did you accept Cliff's proposal in the *first* place?

BOBBI. *Mother* made me do it! I foolishly sent her a snapshot taken of the two of us when we were first going out, and got a mandate to marry Cliff by return mail!

JAKE. But why *obey* your mother's mandate?

REBECCA. (*edge*) Come-come! Surely you don't think Bobbi maintains her extravagant life-style from her piddling income as an *anthropologist*?

ANNABEL. Bobbi! You're marrying *him* for *your* money?!

BOBBI. What *else* could I do? (*falls sobbing into JAKE's eager arms*)

LANGDON. I don't get it?! Mrs. Ralston, why were you so insistent in the *first* place?

REBECCA. Because Cliff bears a remarkable resemblance to my late husband. I felt it was a kind of sign, an omen, as if heaven were *insisting* my daughter marry him! I loved my husband very much. It would be, in a way, like having him *back* again!

CLIFF. That's very flattering. And in a way, rather charming. But I'm sorry—I don't love Bobbi, and she doesn't love me, and we simply won't go *through* with it!

REBECCA. (*edge*) You'd better reconsider. One phone call from me, and Bobbi will be cut off without a penny, and my attorneys will institute a breach-of-promise suit against *you* that will wipe out your good name, career and bank account!

JAKE. (*gently thrusts BOBBI from his enbrace, stands tall, and:*) *No* you won't!

REBECCA. And why *not*?!

JAKE. Because you have no *proof* that the two of them ever *were* engaged to be married!

BOBBI. Jake, what are you saying?

JAKE. Bobbi, in her lackadaisical way, had *me* make all the arrangements for the wedding! The church, the caterer, the works! And I had everything done under Bobbi's name and *mine!*

TRACY. Say, you really *are* some kind of Machiavelli!

BOBBI. (*delighted*) Jake, is this *true?*

JAKE. (*turns to her, takes her hands*) Even that prenuptial thing you signed, *wasn't!* It was an application for a marriage license — because *despite* your power-of-attorney I needed your actual signature on it. The church is booked in *our* name. Even the *honeymoon* tickets are in our name!

CLIFF. I feel like such a fool! Betrayed, deceived and bamboozled by my best friend! (*to JAKE, warmly:*) How can I ever thank you?!

ANNABEL. (*gliding into his arms*) Oh, Cliff, darling, you're *free!*

TRACY. This calls for a celebration!

LANGDON. Then it's the *perfect* time for my *surprise!* (*will turn and Exit* K.R., *fast*)

REBECCA. (*edge*) *Not . . . so . . . fast!* (*when others look her way*) *I* happen to have *proof* of that engagement!

OTHERS. *What* proof?

REBECCA. (*will remove a large envelope from pocket, purse, or wherever*) A photograph of Cliff actually *proposing* to Bobbi!

CLIFF. That's impossible!

BOBBI. Of course it is! I remember the moment in total detail! We were at Elmer and Faleen's pool party—everyone else had gone inside, and right there at poolside Cliff dropped on one knee, won my hand, and slipped the ring on my finger! *Nobody* saw us. So it's *our* word against yours!

REBECCA. Perhaps you two recall a certain *fountain* beside the pool?

CLIFF. Fountain? Do you mean that thing with the statue of *Pan* playing on his *pipes*?

REBECCA. You only *thought* it was Pan playing on his pipes! Actually, it was a *private detective* holding a disguised *camera*!

BOBBI. Mother, you're *joking*!

REBECCA. (*extends envelope*) Am I? Perhaps *this* item will change your mind! (*CLIFF grabs envelope, tears it open*) And don't bother trying to tear it up. I still have the negative in a safe place.

JAKE. Rebecca Ralston, this is *extortion*! Extortion before *witnesses*! I can take you to *court* for this—we have the photo as evidence, and the sworn statement of every person in this room!

REBECCA. Their word — against the word of the third-richest woman on this planet? *Whose* do you think the court will find in *favor* of?

JAKE. (*wilts; to others:*) Hers. It works every time.

ANNABEL. (*looking over CLIFF's shoulder at photograph as he takes it from envelope*) Oh, Cliff, you should be *ashamed* of yourself!

CLIFF. For proposing?

ANNABEL. For getting down on one knee in your Speed-Os!

TRACY. (*taking a look*) You've exposed half your behind!

JAKE. (*looking*) Hey, what's that *on* your behind?

BOBBI. (*looking*) Why, Cliff, you never told me you had a *tattoo*!

REBECCA. *What* tattoo?

CLIFF. I thought you'd *seen* the photograph?

REBECCA. Only the original. I never looked closely at the enlargement.

JAKE. Hey, buddy, why would you get a *hammer and sickle* tattooed on you?

REBECCA. (*gapes, takes a staggering backstep*) Hammer and sickle?! Oh, *nooooo*—! (*flops backward onto sofa in a dead faint*)

CLIFF. (*as he and others rush toward her fallen form*) Oh, great, *now* she thinks I'm a *communist!*

BOBBI. (*on her knees near REBECCA's head*) Smelling salts! Get the smelling salts!

TRACY. (*dryly*) Sorry, but I gave our last bottle to Queen Victoria!

REBECCA. (*coming to*) Oh! What happened? Why am I lying down? (*sights on CLIFF, remembers, sits bolt upright*) Now I remember! (*clutches still-kneeling BOBBI's hand*) My child, you can *not* marry this man!

BOBBI. Mother, don't be an idiot! Clifford Tucker can't *possibly* be a communist!

TRACY. (*with an apartment-encompassing gesture*) Not at *these* prices!

ANNABEL. Cliff, if you're *not* a communist, why *get* a tattoo like that?

CLIFF. It's *not* a tattoo, it's a *birthmark!*

JAKE. But why *keep* it? I mean, buddy, you're a plastic surgeon!

CLIFF. Did *you* ever try performing surgery on your own behind?!

REBECCA. May I *please* get a word in?

OTHERS. *No!*

BOBBI. (*getting to her feet*) I don't understand! Mother's been pushing me for almost a *year* to marry Clifford, and now all at once she's insisting that I *don't!*

ANNABEL. It *is* kind of crazy—I mean, it's not as if the birthmark would show in any of the *wedding*-pictures!

REBECCA. (*stands up*) There won't *be* any wedding-pictures! And *certainly* no *wedding* to this man!

BOBBI. But Mother—not that I *want* to, you understand—but why *can't* I marry Clifford?

REBECCA. (*hesitates a second, steels herself, and then:*) Because he's your *brother*!

OTHERS. *WHAT?!*

REBECCA. (*woefully, wringing her hands, seeking sympathy*) Bobbi's father and I were—very much in love. But the baby was due *long* before our wedding could be arranged. The situation was quite *awkward* in those days. So we handled the whole thing with discretion. Nobody knew. And of course, we had to put our baby up for adoption. I didn't want to—but back in those days, society was composed of mostly *stinkers*! I thought I'd never *see* him again! But now—! Recognizing my baby's *birthmark*—!

CLIFF. (*opens his arms*) *Mother*!

REBECCA. *Son*! (*they embrace*)

BOBBI. Jake! Do you know what this *means*? I'm *free*! (*rushes into his arms*)

JAKE. But only till noon tomorrow! Kiss me, my bride! (*they kiss*)

ANNABEL. (*as he releases REBECCA, she slides into his arms*) Oh, Cliff! It's all so wonderful! Even *without* little Annabel, you'll have enough money to open that clinic *regardless*!

REBECCA. How do you figure?

ANNABEL. Well, as the son of the third-richest woman on this planet—

REBECCA. Listen, honey, I didn't *get* this rich by giving my money *away*! Cliff's inherited my *genes*, not my *assets*!

CLIFF. (*to ANNABEL:*) It's all right, darling. We'll manage. (*they kiss*)

LANGDON. (*emerging* K.D. *with large lidded serving-platter, which he will place at center of dining-table*) Surprise! (*others will turn, then move in that direction curiously*)

REBECCA. I *hope* that's not some more French cuisine—?!

TRACY. Well, it *can't* be a king-size *cheeseburger*—! (*to LANGDON:*) Can it?

ANNABEL. Wait a second—I think I recognize the aroma—it's Beef Wellington!

BOBBI. Oh, I just *adore* Beef Wellington!

LANGDON. Well, then, you're going to be *bananas* about *my* version of the dish! (*reaches for handle of lid*)

CLIFF. You mean it *is* Beef Wellington?

LANGDON. *Almost*—with one ingenious variation!

JAKE. What do you mean?

REBECCA. Yes, what *is* your surprise?

(*All are gathered* U.S. *of table now, looking toward platter, as LANGDON flamboyantly lifts the lid from the platter on his line:*)

LANGDON. *Penguin* Wellington! (*and we see what's apparently a crust-shrouded adult penguin, on its back, easily recognizable because of the up-pointed beak; BOBBI screams and covers her face with her hands*) I *knew* Miss Ralston would be thrilled! [*NOTE: If you want to get elaborate, the penguin sight-gag is even funnier if the sad crust-covered little "corpse" has its "wings" folded upon its breast and holding a short lily.*]

TRACY. Langdon, you twit, what have you *done*?!

LANGDON. I thought Miss Ralston was *crazy* about penguins?

TRACY. As her *ancestors,* not as her *dinner*! (*then all look in amazement as BOBBI — who has been trembling convulsively with her hands over her face — takes her hands away, and we see that her convulsions are from hearty* laughter)

JAKE. Bobbi! You're *laughing*!

ANNABEL. I thought penguins were your *life*?!

BOBBI. That's what I wanted *Cliff* to think! I was so desperate for him to sunder our engagement that I'd try *anything* to push him over the brink! Ye gods, did you really think I *wanted* to honeymoon at the South Pole?!

JAKE. Not to worry. Our travel reservations *are* for the southern hemisphere, but I figured *Tahiti* would be a *nicer* stopoff! (*takes BOBBI in his arms*) See, *I* have this theory that the human race is descended from *coconuts*!

REBECCA. From what *I've* seen of the human race, he may be *right*!

CLIFF. Langdon, where did you *get* a penguin?

LANGDON. I had to improvise — that's what became of all that ground beef! Basically, this is *Meat Loaf* Wellington — (*touches finger to "beak"*) — with a *carrot* on top.

BOBBI. Oh, Annabel, it's short notice, but — will you be in my wedding-party?

ANNABEL. (*shrugs*) Why not! I *already* look like a *wedding-cake*!

REBECCA. And Clifford — son — as soon as you set the date for *your* wedding, let me know. I *must* give you a wedding present suitable to your status in society!

CLIFF. (*thinks a second; then:*) How about the Bank of America?

REBECCA. (*takes his hand*) You've got a deal!

LANGDON. Hey, the *time*! (*starts toward foyer, others trailing more slowly after him*) I've got an *acting*-class in fifteen minutes!

REBECCA. Tell the teacher to work on your French accent!

LANGDON. (*stops just above sofa area*) Oh, we're not doing *vocal* stuff tonight. We're concentrating on *mime*.

CLIFF. You mean where the performer .spends the *entire* evening not saying a *word*?

JAKE. Maybe you should take *Bobbi* with you!

TRACY. (*heading for bar*) Wait, you can't go *yet*! We've got to drink a *toast* to the happy occasion!

LANGDON. (*moving to help her at bar, where they'll get seven stemmed glasses of wine onto a tray over the next few speeches*) It's *only* a *mime* class—

TRACY. I mean *this* happy occasion—Jake's marrying Bobbi, Cliff's found his real-life mother—

ANNABEL. There's finally a buyer for little Annabel—

CLIFF. (*slips an arm around her*) —and a taker for *big* Annabel!

REBECCA. And I've found my long-lost child—

LANGDON. —and I've found an apartment—

TRACY. (*as she and LANGDON come down to group and distribute glasses*) —and I've finally landed Prince Charming—

LANGDON. I thought you liked *me*?

JAKE. That *is* you!

BOBBI. (*raises her glass*) Well, here's to a happy wedding— (*NOTE: Each speaker will raise his/her glass on spoken lines:*)

JAKE. And here's farewell to those penguins—

CLIFF. And here's to the sales on little Annabel—

ANNABEL. And here's to my super-ingenious father—

TRACY. And here's to the Village Voice advertisement—

LANGDON. And here's to amputating that monkey's tail—

REBECCA. And here's to that wonderful little hammer-and-sickle birthmark — (*and then as all raise their glasses to their lips, REBECCA hesitates, lowers her glass slightly, and ponders aloud:*) —or was it a *skull-and-crossbones?!* (*and as others all lower their glasses and stare at her in the onset of horrified consternation—*)

THE CURTAIN FALLS

End of Show

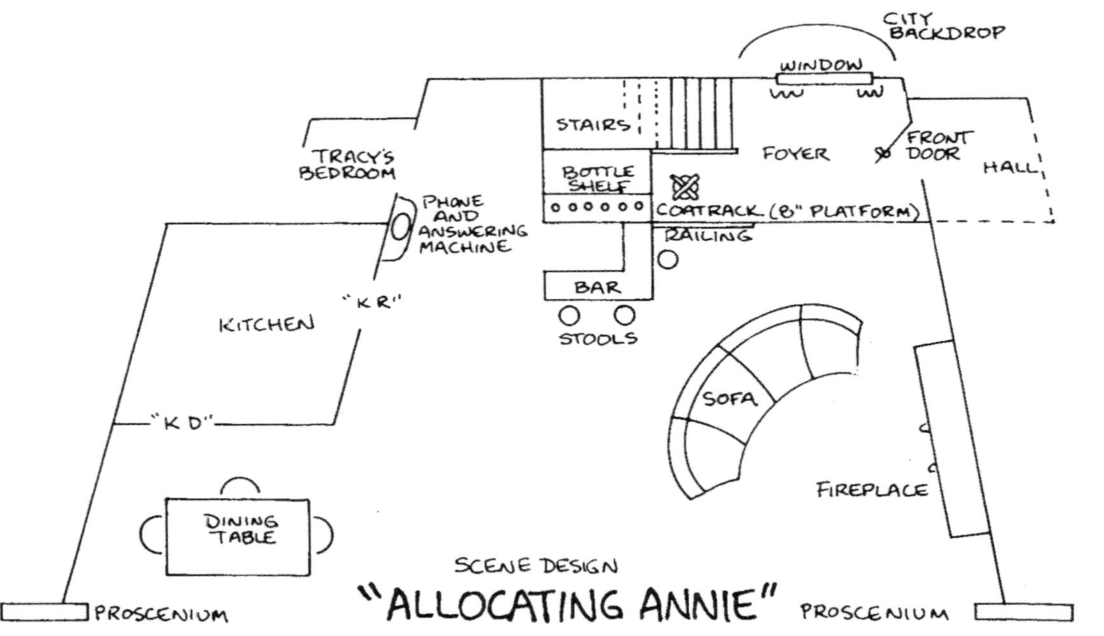

CITY BACKDROP
WINDOW
STAIRS
FOYER
FRONT DOOR
HALL
TRACY'S BEDROOM
BOTTLE SHELF
COATRACK (8" PLATFORM)
PHONE AND ANSWERING MACHINE
RAILING
BAR
STOOLS
"K R"
KITCHEN
"K D"
SOFA
FIREPLACE
DINING TABLE
PROSCENIUM
PROSCENIUM
SCENE DESIGN
"ALLOCATING ANNIE"

16